W9-AOM-075

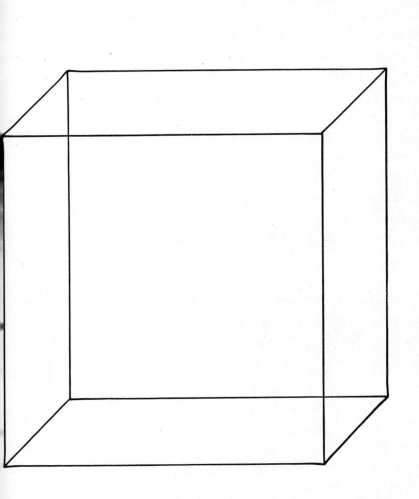

New Worlds of Science Fiction

Edited by Roger Elwood

 M. EVANS AND COMPANY, INC. / NEW YORK, N.Y. 10017

M. Evans and Company titles are distributed in
the United States by the J. B. Lippincott Company,
East Washington Square, Philadelphia, Pa. 19105;
and in Canada by McClelland & Stewart Ltd.,
25 Hollinger Road, Toronto M4B 3G2, Ontario

Library of Congress Cataloging in Publication Data

Main entry under title:

Tomorrow: new worlds of science fiction.

    CONTENTS: Holly, J. H. Come see the last man cry.—
Nourse, A. E. Nize Kitty.—Hoskins, R. The Kelly's
eye. [etc.]
    1. Science fiction. [1. Science fiction.
2. Short stories] I. Elwood, Roger.
PZ5.T62   [Fic]   75-17783
ISBN 0-87131-185-2

Copyright © 1975 by Roger Elwood
All rights reserved under International and Pan-
American Copyright Conventions

Designed by Joel Schick

Manufactured in the United States of America

9 8 7 6 5 4 3 2 1

Contents

Preface

Science fiction is a genre of the imagination to a far greater degree than any other literary category. By its very nature it provides an escape to frontiers which are not yet in existence or, at least, which are unknown.

The stories in this anthology are brand-new; each has been written especially for *Tomorrow*. Most of the authors are experienced professionals; a few are newcomers who nevertheless have something to say and the ability to say it.

You will find action-adventure herein: "The Kelly's Eye" by Robert Hoskins; "Castle in the Stars" by Terry Carr.

There are social commentary vehicles in this anthology: "Come See the Last Man Cry" by Joan Hunter Holly; "Nize Kitty" by Alan E. Nourse.

You can read semi-experimental stories also: "Journey of the Soul" by Neil Shapiro is an example. If you like warm, sentimental stories, you'll enjoy "Perihesperon" by Greg Bear. There is science fiction fantasy: "Enchanté" by Andrew J. Offutt.

And much more. You can read three other stories herein: "Arctic Rescue" by John Keith Mason; "Always Somebody There" by Brian W. Aldiss; and, "Death or Consequences" by Sonya Dorman.

We have tried, as a key consideration, to pick variety and quality.

ROGER ELWOOD

Linwood, N.J.

COME SEE THE LAST MAN CRY

by Joan Hunter Holly

T TEN O'CLOCK, every seat in the auditorium was filled. Row after row of people sat there, dressed alike in the fashionable Coverall style, with only the varying colors to set them apart as individuals. They waited expectantly, the sound of them a steady drone, their attention seldom veering from the wall that would soon "melt" away and show them the interior of Peter's playroom.

Frederic Dainig stood near the front, the earphones of his headset sensitive to the noises going on inside the playroom. He was the only human being in the world privy to those sounds at the moment. He was waiting, too—for the moment when he had to judge the ultimate second, and then with a hand signal, alert the men behind the cameras. The same signal would set the engineers in motion. Flicking some switches, they would transform the solid wall into transparent nothingness and reveal Peter to the audience and to the TV world.

He didn't understand how the "melting" was accomplished. While it rendered Peter naked to the audience, it left the blank yellow wall in his playroom blank and yellow for him. The boy had no idea that any of this went on three times a day. He wouldn't comprehend it, anyway. His Moron's mind wasn't capable of anything but the simplest directions or the most basic feelings.

Dainig waited restlessly for the Viewing to begin, bored with the routine, but staying alert so he wouldn't miss his cue. He was the key to everything. Nothing would happen until the drop of his signaling hand, and that, in turn, depended on the desired reaction in the boy. Peter always flashed before the public in full-blown emotion. Only Dainig, Dr. Cooper, and Dr. Mattison knew what it took to bring that emotion about. A young man, himself—barely thirty, and plucked prematurely from his training as an Anti-Emotion Conditioner—Dainig hoped that one day he could manipulate a Viewing Child as expertly as the two Doctors, who were his immediate superiors.

A sudden crack of new sound in his earphones rushed him to his assigned position. Until now, there had only been the echo of Peter, as he bounced his big red ball and hummed a tuneless melody. Now, the thump of footsteps interrupted the rhythm of the ball. They marked the entrance of Cooper and Mattison into Peter's playroom, and Dainig stiffened, ready to signal the technicians.

"How are you today, Peter?" he heard Clara Mattison ask.

"I'm playing ball. Do you want to catch it?" Peter's voice was frail against hers.

"We're here to talk to you," Dr. Cooper's deeper tones came through. "We want to talk about your Mama and Daddy."

"No, please. I want to play with the ball." Peter was shying from the subject. A good sign.

"Did you tell your Mama 'No,' too? Is that what made her stop loving you, Peter?" Dr. Mattison asked. "Were you a bad boy?"

"Never. I was always good. I love her."

"But, she doesn't love you, does she? If she did, she would be here with you. You must have been a very bad boy."

"But I wasn't!" Peter was defiant. Dainig could visualize the way his pointed chin must be sticking out. The boy didn't like the two doctors and made no pretenses about it. "You just be quiet, Matty, because you're not nice to say that. I got lost from her—from Daddy, too. I just can't find them, anymore. But, I'm good. I'm special! Danny says so."

Cooper took over, reinforcing Mattison. "Do you remember your Mama, Peter? Do you remember what she looked like? How warm she was when she held you?"

There was a brief silence, then Peter broke it, his voice higher. "I remember the way she smells! I like that. I want her to come back. Can you tell her where I am?"

"She doesn't want to know. You're lost, and she's glad of it. You can't ever see her again, because you were bad." Cooper was playing on Peter's greatest single worry—that he had *caused* his separation from his parents. "Very bad."

"Was I? But—how? I'm sorry, Mama. Please, Matty—I want her. Tell her to love me even if I'm bad. I need her to."

The child was starting to whimper and his breath to gasp. Dainig could clearly imagine the tears wetting his eyes, and for some ungodly reason, hated his *own* eyes for remaining dry.

Mattison edged in the final knife. "Do you want her to hold you in her arms again? To cuddle you, and sing to you?"

"Oh, yes—please!" Peter cried, eager with the visions

Mattison was planting in his senses. "I remember . . . Can she, Matty?"

Dainig raised his hand, preparing to give the Viewing signal. The audience saw his movement and leaned forward.

"Can she?" Peter begged. "Will you tell her to come, Matty?"

"Well, now . . . If . . ."

There was another silence. Dainig knew that Mattison was eyeing the boy, her face impassive as she measured the seconds to give him time to believe she was going to say, "Yes."

Then her voice emerged harsh and brittle. "No, Peter! You can want her with all of your heart, but you'll never see her again. Do you understand? *Never!*"

"But she *has* to love me, and—she *wants*—and . . . " Peter was drowned in confusion, his Moron's brain tangled in itself. At last it gave way to the only thing it possessed. Emotion. And the cry that carried his last, "Matty! *Please*, Matty!" was a broken wail.

The Doctors' footsteps rushed away and full-throated sobs began in Dainig's ears just as his hand arced down the Viewing signal. The wall "melted," and there was Peter, bent double on his knees, his shoulders racking, his hands clutched to his face, his sobs of "Mama! Please come and find me, Mama!" now audible over the loudspeaker, carrying to every ear in the auditorium and to every TV receiver eavesdropping on his pain.

A whisper came out of the audience. "Look how hard he's crying. Poor Peter."

"And, without drugs!" another whisper answered.

Dainig pulled off his earphones and watched the spectacle firsthand. The crowd strained forward, absorbing Peter's emotion avidly, fascinated, envious, and held there by a touch of something too intense to explain.

Peter was on his feet, now, swiveling around in a futile attempt to find Mattison and Cooper. But they had retreated, and he was totally alone with his grief, with no one to give comfort. His face ran with tears, and his pale yellow hair was separating into damp straggles across his forehead, making his delicate skin look florid from the paroxysms of despair and wanting. His hands had nowhere to go, and grabbed at the air in impotent fists.

An unsought image of the way Peter had been at breakfast jumped into Dainig's mind. Thoroughly happy, the child had bounced about the playroom, flinging himself against Dainig, and experimenting with changing, "I like you, Danny," to "I love you."

Dainig gave credit to Mattison and Cooper. They played Peter expertly. Their years of erasing children's emotions were now turned into tools for stimulating Peter's. He provided them with the keys to Peter's moods, but they triggered the emotions. And they never failed.

"But, are we right? Since Peter has the capacity to be happy, is it right for us to torment him into Unhappiness?"

Dainig twitched at the intrusion. What had engendered that question?

He knew without asking a second time. It had been thrust up from the anxiety that had dogged him for weeks. It came from a job that demanded twelve hours a day from him. It festered from spending too much time with Peter.

He deliberately set his conscious mind to give a proper answer, lecturing himself. "Peter's entire reason for being alive is to perform Emotion. There is no right and no wrong to it. Even if there might be, it's Peter's life and Peter's problem. *I* don't care, one way or the other."

The positive statement did little to help him, because it shouldn't have been necessary in the first place. These odd attacks were coming too often. He knew he needed some time to himself, but taking a leave was impossible. Peter merited no vacations, so neither did his Companion.

Dainig retreated by turning his back to the Viewing wall. He would see Peter flesh-to-flesh all too soon. He would even have to hold that quivering little body in his arms while he dammed-up Peter's emotions during the time between this Viewing and the next.

He closed his ears to Peter's cries and put his mind on the audience, satisfied from their expressions that they were receiving what they deserved. A good performance. Even Peter's mother, sitting proudly in the front row, was gobbling down the sobs. She had been all too glad to relinquish her job as his Custodian when the previous Viewing Child had been destroyed and the Center had sent for Peter. Nevertheless, she came regularly to enjoy her own share of vicarious emotion, and her face today said that this Viewing was a success.

Two days later, Dainig balanced Peter's breakfast tray gingerly as he entered the child's three-room Complex by way of the concealed door in the playroom. Peter's toys were all neatly in their box, and the two chairs and low table were dusted and gleaming, as proof that the Service people had been on the job during the night. The room was brightly decorated with brown carpet, orange floor pillows, and yellow walls. Even the front "wall-that-wasn't-a-wall" —the one that opened into the auditorium—appeared to be yellow, although devoid of any pictures or ornaments.

Dainig set the breakfast tray on the table in Peter's tiny bedroom, then switched on the lights. Peter was a little hump under the covers, lying deathly still in a pretense of sleep so he could play his favorite game of "Fooling Danny."

Dainig played along. "Morning Peter! Let's have those sleepy eyes open before I count to three. One . . . two . . ."

Peter heaved himself upright, his pale hair making a fringe over his brown eyes, his mouth wide in a triumphant grin. "I wasn't even asleep! I fooled you again, Danny!"

To sustain their running joke, Dainig plopped on the bed and wrestled him around until Peter squealed, then shooed him into the bathroom for his morning scrubbing, all the while marveling at the boy's thin body and short stature. A boy of eight should be bigger than this. But Peter's body remained as backward and limited as his brain.

When he was at last dressed in a bright-red Coverall, Peter swooped down on the breakfast tray and lifted the metal covers, yelping, "Eggs! Danny, did you see I got eggs?"

"I did. And you'd better eat them fast, or I'll do it, myself. I don't taste real eggs very often."

Peter was willing, and Dainig was relieved. The child had suffered through two days of Crying Viewings now, and they always robbed his frail body of the strength it needed to grow and support him. But, Peter ate quickly this morning, chattering as he always did when his world was good. Danny's presence seemed to be the ingredient for making it good.

"My Mama used to make food like this in the kitchen. Do you have a kitchen?" Peter asked him. "I had one. I even had a window. In that other place I was. I could look out and see the street and the people. Have you ever seen the street, Danny?"

"I have."

"Is it still there? I think maybe it went away. I can't see it, so it went away. It died—just like my fish—and I can't see it, anymore."

"Whatever you say, Peter. Now, if you're through eating, let's go to the playroom and find some of your toys."

He trailed after the child's awkward run, satisfied to

see it. The last two days had worn on his own stamina, as he calmed Peter's tears over and over again. Today, since the boy was happy, he might not have to do it.

The first half of the two-hour play period passed normally as Peter tossed his big, soft ball, then drew pictures of his fish and tried to color them. He couldn't stay inside the lines, and as his enthusiasm ebbed, he began to peer at Dainig, wanting to say something, but backing off.

"What's wrong?" Dainig asked, when one of the brown stares lasted an uncomfortably long time. "You can tell me."

Peter sighed. "It's just . . . I like you, Danny. Mostly, I feel lonely, but when you come, it's all right, and I love you. Can't you be with me more? I don't like to be alone."

"I'm here six hours every day, and you have Coop and Matty, too."

"I don't like Coop and Matty. Sometimes they're mean. My Mama never left me all alone. We looked out the window. And then Daddy came, and we played."

"Things have changed, Peter. I've told you before."

"I know. I'm a special boy, now. You said so, but I don't see why."

Dainig had explained it a hundred times, but did it again, aware that Peter never understood half of what he said. "You're special because you're different from everyone else. You have the ability to *feel* things, Peter. You have emotions, and no one else has those. You can laugh and cry and love."

"That's *easy*, that's not special," Peter objected. "You can do it, too. You can laugh, too, can't you, Danny?"

"Have you ever seen me do it?"

Peter thought for a long moment. "No. But you could if you wanted to."

"No, Peter. I can't. Not on my own. I have to take drugs

to do it, and then I know that the drugs are causing it, so it's not real. You cry and feel unhappy without drugs. That's why you're special."

"I don't like to cry," Peter said, soberly. "I'd rather laugh."

"Of course. But you have to do both in order to demonstrate full human emotion."

Peter didn't understand the large words, but shrugged his inability aside. "Is Love one of those things? I love a lot. I love you, and Mama and Daddy. Only—I never see them anymore, and . . ."

Dainig moved fast to make him stop. He was heading into tears, and that kind of emotion couldn't be wasted without a Viewing audience. "Don't think about your parents if it makes you unhappy. Think about something nice."

"I can't just make it stop and start. And I don't *have* anything nice. I can't remember what bad things I did to make my Mama stop loving me. Do you know?" His brown eyes were growing misty.

"Stop it!" Dainig commanded. "She would love you if she could, but I've told you over and over again why she can't. And why your Daddy can't. They're dead. Like your goldfish is dead." The Doctors didn't like him to say that, but Dainig couldn't see that it had ever made any difference to their work with Peter.

It proved to be a mistake, anyway. Peter's tears were more imminent than ever. Dainig grabbed the first happy thing he could bring to mind. "How would you like to have another goldfish?"

Peter immediately turned eager. "Could I? Is there another fish?"

"Lots of them. I'll see if Matty and Coop will let you have one."

"Will you *really* ask them, Danny? I love my fish. Will you? So they'll quit being mean to me every day?"

Dainig stared at him, weighing the good of it, then made up his mind. "I promise, little boy. I'll ask them."

Peter rushed against his legs and clung like a two-pronged magnet. "Will you *make* them do it? For *me*?"

"I'll give it everything I've got in me, Peter. I'll even argue for you." That was a dangerous prospect, but he meant it, and his last, decisive, "I promise," was squashed under the force of Peter's squeal of delight.

There was no way to battle the child's excitement, so Dainig rolled with it, lifting him off his feet to twirl him in a circle, then plopping him on the floor when he tickled him until he giggled. As Peter quickly wore himself out, Dainig shunted his mind to a new subject. "That's enough noise for right now. Let's play with your Jack-in-the-box. I'll bet you can't tell when it's going to pop up."

Peter went dutifully to get his toy, and Dainig heaved a sigh. He had performed his job doubly well this morning. He had *two* possibilities to report to the Doctors: that Peter was still ripe for another attack of Grief, or that Peter could be made to display Happiness by the restoration of his pet fish. The Doctors usually kept Peter crying as long as his tears would fall, and disputing them was never wise. Yet . . .

The queer anxiety leaped inside him, full force, but he ignored it for once. Peter had an inborn right to a few days of joy.

When his two hours with Peter ticked out, Dainig distracted the child and effected his exit through the concealed door in the bathroom. He started down the corridor to give his morning report to the Doctors, tensed for a possible argument, his body trying to change his mind by screaming out how tired it was. Peter precipitated exhaustion in him, lately.

He didn't dare let it show. The Doctors had to believe that everything was normal—and for more than one reason. His position as Peter's Companion, yes. But there was another motive inside him. One he failed to pin down, and that warned, *"Don't try."*

He valiantly put a lightness in his long stride that made his brown forelock bounce with every step. He only wished his spirit were that bouncy.

Both Doctors were waiting in Cooper's office, Cooper's fifty years visible on his empty face, his gray hair lending him a badge of experience which he valued. Clara Mattison was dressed in her usual somber-gray Coverall. A plumpish woman, she might have resembled the old word "matronly" if she had possessed anything of the necessary ample warmth. But there was none of that in Peter's Matty. There was only aloof science and devotion to her work.

At first sight of Dainig, she accused, "You are five minutes late, young man. We expect *you* to wait for *us*, not the other way around."

"Yes, Dr. Mattison. I'm sorry."

"Is something wrong with Peter?" Cooper asked anxiously.

"Peter is fine. A little tired, but fine. He's actually quite happy this morning, except for the fact that I think he's too lonely." Dainig had grabbed his chance boldly.

"That's preposterous," Dr. Cooper said. "You're with him six hours a day."

"A day is a great deal longer than six hours, sir. He was never left alone before he came here. He had his parents, and a pet goldfish, and . . ."

"This addition of figures bothers you, does it?" Mattison interrupted before he had reached his purpose in bringing it up.

He dodged. "I only wondered if loneliness couldn't be bad for his emotional health. It might deaden him."

"You have it entirely backward," Cooper said, curtly. Neither one of them was a patient teacher. "He is quiescent when he's alone. That makes his response more vigorous when we approach him before the Viewings."

"But he's such a *little* boy, sir. Mentally, I mean. Shouldn't even a *normal* child have more than six hours of company?"

"You're saying we should pamper him," Dr. Mattison snorted. "By no means. It is our responsibility to care *for* him, not about him. To see to his physical needs, and that is all. I'm amazed that you require a lesson in this, Dainig. Peter is deliberately kept lonely so he will react when we assault him with kindness or abuse. Our presence focuses his attention and shocks him. Why do you think you are excluded from the Viewing warm-ups? Simply because, as his Companion, you cannot elicit the shock response we force out of him."

Her gaze fastened on him harshly, too harshly to be the result of what he had said. She harbored some hidden reason. He didn't duel with Dr. Mattison. She was too avid, too sharp, and the two of them had never struck an easy relationship. He always edged around her by feigning deference, and he followed that route now.

"Of course," he said. "I'm sorry I showed my ignorance."

"Nonsense," Cooper stated. "How else can you learn, young man? But, get on with your report. You were telling us about Peter's mood."

Dainig cleared his throat and plunged in again, determined to lead them his way. "He's lonely, as I said, but totally contented otherwise. The two factors offer us a good way into him. If we fill that loneliness for the moment, we can draw a fine performance from him. I propose that we give him a goldfish. Like the one he owned at home. He only had three things in the world to call his own, and the goldfish was one of them. He held it as dearly as he held his parents."

"You're advising us to turn him Happy again?" The edge on Mattison's voice didn't match her placid face. "After we've worked so hard to set him crying?"

"We've shown him crying for two days," Dainig pointed out.

"Not nearly long enough," Cooper sided with Mattison. "The audiences aren't sated, yet."

"Is there *no* opportunity to keep him in the depressed state?" Mattison demanded.

"I can only report what I see, and he has overcome his grief—for the moment. You know how suddenly his moods change." He threw in an extra stumbling block for them, remembering his promise to Peter. "Getting him to cry today would mean a lengthy warm-up. On the other hand, if we go *with* his mood, he'll come back to his parents as a matter of course. He always does."

Cooper fell silent, weighing the extra time against the result. Dainig sensed victory.

Mattison cast her empty gaze on Cooper, and insisted, "Happiness will not do! The audience deserves its full measure, Doctor. I know how you dislike using pain to force tears, since it reveals 'reaction' and not emotion, but I insist on *sobs* out of that Defective while he still has water enough in him to cry!"

"You're right. He owes the people a good performance," Cooper parroted his partner.

"But, he was so contented this morning . . ." Dainig's voice gave out, as he physically felt the clutch of Mattison's eyes. She stared at him without blinking, probing deep.

"What is it you want from him, Dainig?" she asked. "If Peter does not have this special use in the world, then he has *none*. He is defective. His only alternative to Performing is destruction. That will come soon enough when he catches on to our manipulation. So, what is it that you want? His death? Now?"

"Hardly, Dr. Mattison. I'd be out of a job. But, why does he have to continue with the crying right now? We'll have him back to it soon enough. Why can't he enjoy . . . ? I told you he's lost weight. Can't we leave him alone for a few days?"

Her eyes slitted. "What sort of question was that, Dainig? It verges on concern for the boy."

Dainig's very skin contracted. "No!—of course not! It . . ." He flailed about for an excuse. "It was actually selfish. When Peter cries, it's harder on me. I'm particularly tired right now, and . . ." He was squirming, and she knew it. Her stare wouldn't relent, so he admitted his discomfort with it, trying to lead her away from the truth. "I certainly didn't intend to put myself under fire."

"I'm not saying anything as drastic as that. Yet. I'm simply checking on you, Dainig. You spend six hours every day with raw emotion, and that can have insidious effects on a man. Even—pray not!—Reemergence. It is my duty to watch you. You've been a bit 'off' lately. Slower in your reflexes, and generally operating at a low level. You have to admit that your behavior is aberrant this morning. You were late—you brought up that strange notion of loneliness —and you have an overall attitude of . . ."

"Weariness," Dainig hurried to defend himself. "I just confessed to being tired. I'll try to correct it."

"We have no time to fret about Dainig," Cooper blessedly inserted his voice. "There's a Viewing schedule to be met." He sighed oddly, and looked to Dr. Mattison. "The last suggestion was pain. So, it's only a matter of what kind, and what instrument."

With the threat of pain rushing at Peter, Dainig forced his brain to find a solution—for both of them. "I don't want to see that," he opposed the Doctors. "And, I'm not being out of order. I just have a better idea. The goldfish can be used two ways, remember. *For* Peter, or *against* him. All you need to do is remind Peter of how much he loved his pet, and that it was his only friend. He really thought it was, you know. Then, when you have him deep inside that warm memory, hit him with the fact that he'll never see it again. He'll give us our performance."

Mattison's lips fairly smacked at the notion. "I should have considered this line, myself. Fine! We'll work in that direction then, Dr. Cooper. And, Dainig—be prepared to earn your allotment today, because it *is* going to be a Crying session, whether you agree or not."

"Whatever is best for the audience," he said, docilely. "I really don't disagree, you know."

On those words, he left the office. There was nothing more he dared to say. He was defenseless against her ferreting mind, and she had abruptly changed from his watchdog into a terrier, holding him and shaking him to dislodge any possible flaw. The danger lay in his free-floating anxiety. It told him that he might have such a flaw.

He put it out of his mind. The whole idea of endangering himself because a child was lonely reeked of foolishness, anyway. He had no foundation for thinking he understood how Peter felt, when he couldn't "feel," himself.

Peter cried over the goldfish for two long days, and the plan for the third was more of the same. Dainig came close to damning the boy for letting the Doctors hack him to pieces over a bowl of water with a scaley carp inside it. So Peter "loved" his fish! Just what was Love? Dainig didn't know, and had no inclination to find out. All he could see was that this new day promised him no relief.

So, when his former classmate, Sam Richmond, collared him before Peter's breakfast, he surrendered his free hour and let Rich lead him through the Anti-Emotion Conditioning Center on what he hoped wouldn't be a futile trip. He needed something to fill his mind. Something besides the anxiety which threatened to consume him. The worst part of it was that the anxiety had no specific focus. Since he couldn't find its cause, he had to escape from it.

The corridor swarmed with students arrowing for early classes. As Dainig struggled to keep abreast of Richmond, the bump and brush of their bodies was an unexpected annoyance. Normally, he didn't notice it as anything more than a part of everyday living.

Displeased with what the commotion was doing to him, he edged closer to Richmond, shouting to be heard above the noise. "I don't think I should take time for this, after all, Rich. It sounded good, but . . . I enjoy my hour of quiet in the morning."

"No arguments, friend," Richmond answered. "You're *gray* this morning, Dainig, and I believe you need the Clinic's stimulation. I'm going to see that you get it. How long has it been since you've stopped in to observe?"

"Too long," Dainig admitted. "I don't have time. Work comes first." He wanted no discussion of his down mood, no pointing-up of his intensely personal problems. They were his secret—although it seemed that other people were beginning to notice. "Being Peter's Companion eats up my days."

Richmond walked on, stubborn and determined. "Not this one. *I* have a hand in this one, friend."

Dainig wished the man would stop using that term. They had been competitors once, but never friends, so it dropped out of his mouth with no meaning.

At the end of the corridor, where the bank of elevators blinked with their "UP" and "DOWN" lights, they had a long wait. At this time of day, ninety-nine percent of them were "Express-Up," since the classrooms were located on the upper floors. When one finally blinked "DOWN," and gaped for them, they were the only two who entered.

"We're out of the mob, at least," Dainig said, gratefully.

"You don't like crowds anymore, *either*? It's only been a few weeks since I've seen you, but you make it seem like a year! I can't anticipate any of your reactions."

"I'm in the same position with you," Dainig confessed, as the car started its slow trip. It would halt at every one of the twelve floors, but if they were lucky, no one else would get on. "Now that I've dropped my classes to take over with Peter, I don't even know how to make decent conversation with you. How far along are you in your classwork, anyway?"

"Practically finished with it. I've started in the Clinic, itself. Working with the children."

"You're a Technician's Aide, already?"

"If you'd keep in touch, you'd realize that's just normal progression. I didn't accelerate, or anything. I'm only an Aide, but it's close to the real thing, so I think you'll be interested in what I'm doing. My case right now is Affection-and-Love Removal in a four-year-old girl. She's about in the middle of her course, so she is still being motivated with her favorite doll. By the time she left yesterday, she didn't even want to *touch* that doll. After today's session, she won't care if we tear it to pieces. And it used to be her prized possession."

"You'll start on animate things next, I suppose."

"Probably tomorrow. She has a puppy, so we'll use that. Plus her parents—naturally. She won't have any Affection left in her by the end of the month."

"You've gone so far. I envy you, Rich. My training was cut off so abruptly . . ."

"Don't envy me until you've tried it for yourself. I'm not all that satisfied, anymore."

The final stop of the elevator spared Dainig from delving

into that statement. Richmond strode forward, but Dainig only tagged along through the empty hallway.

Noticing it, Richmond swiveled to stare at him. "I tell you, Dainig, you're in bad shape. Are you coming with me to the Clinic, or aren't you?"

"Maybe it . . ." Dainig started to back off.

"I say you *are*," Richmond was suddenly authoritative. "*If* you'll make the effort to move your feet."

Dainig increased his pace, wondering where Richmond had learned this self-confidence. Or had Rich always been this way? And had he, himself, once been Richmond's match? If so, something had interposed itself.

One of the Clinic doors loomed beside them, marked "AGE FOUR." Richmond touched the handle and glanced over his shoulder to ask, "Ready?" He scowled. "Why the look of apprehension?"

"You're misreading exhaustion-caused anxiety."

"Well, here's your remedy. The best answer for exhaustion is stimulation. You're going to use this hour to get back to your career, and change some of this gray mood into pride in yourself."

Dainig nodded dully. "You sound like Dr. Cooper."

"Someday I may *be* Dr. Cooper." With that coded remark, Richmond opened the door and led the way inside.

The vast room was a maze of wide aisles spaced between double rows of cubicles. And it was alive with sound. Four-year-old children sat in the cubicles, one to a unit, their heads fitted with electrode-caps containing brain-wave sensors, their small bodies dripping wires that measured heartbeat, blood pressure, skin temperature and respiration.

Some were viewing full-color pictures that flashed on screens in front of them: pictures of their parents, their siblings, their homes. Others faced low tables that held objects: sometimes a doll, sometimes a stuffed toy, and sometimes a pet animal—any especially loved or feared object that was part of their lives.

Technicians strode up and down the aisles, busily checking the Read-Out rectangles beside each cubicle. Here and there, they halted to replace an object or to deliberately tempt a child to reach for a doll or react to a picture. They were the mobile, skilled hands of the Monitoring Computer. The Machine, itself, was responsible for the constant sound of the room.

It was a sound composed of gasps, of startled cries, of brief pain, and sometimes of wails for "Mama," as the Computer sent its measured sonic and electric shocks into the small bodies to wash them clean of Affection, Hatred, and Love. A significant change in brain waves or a rise in pulse-rate—any giveaway sign of emotion—was answered by shock, until the child learned to curb the emotion and eradicate it from his soul. If the child didn't, the lessons went on, their frequency increased. Emotion was shock-conditioned out of them, as it must be, to insure their survival in a world which otherwise could only produce nervous collapse. None of the AEC process was painful to the point of actual suffering. It was based on Fear—one emotion the child could keep forever.

Dainig paced beside Richmond and watched the children undergo the procedure, but failed to raise the change of mental attitude he had come to find. AEC's purpose was wholly humanitarian, and he appreciated that fact. He even experienced a renewed sense of awe at its operation. It was so delicate and precise that it could turn out a child capable of feeling nothing except Anxiety, Pride, Irritation, and Fear—the four emotions necessary to keep a citizen safe, on his toes, and productive.

Yet, today, his mind obstinately refused to focus on the good. Instead, it made him sorely aware that every one of these children carried the potential of Peter—minus Peter's crippled IQ, of course. They had all been laughing, crying, smiling human beings before they began their sessions. They never would be again.

"That's all for their own good," he reminded himself, wondering why he thought about it at all. He didn't "care" that they were losing their inborn abilities. He didn't have it in him to "care." Not since he, himself, had passed this way when *he* was four years old.

Without warning, Richmond stopped walking. He stood still in the aisle, sweeping his gaze slowly back and forth. From this particular spot, they could see into four cubicles at once, watch four children doing four entirely different things, and the sight was affecting Rich in some odd way.

When he finally spoke, his voice was pitched at a confidential level. "We both have problems, Dainig. Mine is disenchantment. I don't find what I need in here, anymore. Since I actually started working, I've come to think that Technicians are nothing but cogs in the Machine, and *it* runs the Clinic. They're only secondary memory-tapes—or scanners to check the Read-Outs. I want to be more active. To take more pride in what I do."

Dainig stared at him with as much amazement as he could ever muster. "How? You're talking impossibilities. The AEC method is locked-in to a tested procedure. A Technician can only do limited . . ."

"I mean *Re*-conditioning."

Dainig stiffened. He didn't like that word. "You're not serious."

"Entirely. Reconditioning is active. You set the gauges, yourself, and measure out the pain, yourself. All the Machine does is indicate when it's needed. The roles are reversed."

Dainig stepped a pace away from him. "I don't believe

this! You could never consciously inflict that kind of pain! The stories I've heard about the Reconditioning Labs . . . Uh-uh."

"The stories are true. I've spent time there observing, so I know from experience. You don't hear gasps coming from those cells. You hear agony! It's severe, and it's fast, and it's active, and the more I see of it, the less I'm fulfilled by this place. Once I saw the possibilities in actually *doing* the work, *sending* the shocks. . . ."

"How far has this gone with you?"

"I've filed a tentative application for transfer."

Dainig hurried away from that answer, walking on down the aisle. "You're talking about sadism. You've gotten your values confused."

"It is not sadism! Putting a Reemerger on the right track is a higher form of mercy than what is going on around us right now."

"But, it's done so brutally. Brainwashing. Pain!"

"Naturally it's brutal. You can't handle an adult the way you do a child. It's painful, but fast. And the faster the better. You'd understand that if you had ever seen the hell-ridden people waiting in those detention cells for their next treatment. It would only be sadistic if you extended their condition for years. Mankind cannot live with emotions."

"All right, Rich, I can't argue. I've never gone near the Labs. But, I'd think it over very hard, if I were you."

"I've done just that. And I have an idea that I've already made up my mind."

They had reached the far end of the vast room, and Richmond hushed until they were outside in the deserted hallway. Then, he switched the subject entirely. He looked at Dainig with bright, probing eyes, and said, "You don't appear any better for your trip through the Clinic. Didn't it help you at all?"

"Not when you throw plans like training to be a Reconditioner at me."

"My ears say that's only an excuse, friend. There's something on your mind. So, how about a cup of coffee and a talk?"

"I don't have time. Peter needs his breakfast."

"*After* Peter's breakfast, then. I'm determined to resurrect the Dainig I used to know, and I won't listen to excuses. In fact, if I hear any more, I'm going to leap to some strange conclusions."

"What do you mean by that?" Dainig jerked with anxiety.

"Meet me later and find out. If you need to talk, I have a willing ear. If you need to be talked *to*, I have the words. Are you going to say 'yes'? Or do I start digging for those conclusions?"

Dainig's anxiety unaccountably churned into Fear. Richmond meant every word he was saying, and something in that fact cried out, "Danger!" *Why?* He didn't know why, and the dangling question made him sure he shouldn't tarry with the man.

"There's no way," he insisted. "I go straight to Cooper and Mattison when I leave Peter."

"That shuts me out, then. Do it when you can, though, Dainig. You need it. Oh—before I forget—thanks for this last week of Viewings. Is he going to cry again today?"

"You, too? Dainig sighed. "And here I'm doing everything I can to reschedule some Happy Viewings. They make less work for me. I'd just as soon have him happy all the time."

"That would defeat his purpose. He has to give people what they need. Don't push too hard to reschedule him, friend."

With that, Richmond strode away, leaving Dainig with an

odd sensation of standing totally alone. Was he the *only* one, then?

He forced his feet toward the kitchen where Peter's meals were prepared, reprimanding himself for being out of step. What Richmond had said was not callous. It was true.

By the time he picked up Peter's tray, he believed it.

The next morning, Dainig was again standing beside an audience, waiting to signal the Viewing. He wasn't uneasy about this one, for it was to be a Happy Viewing. He had personally bought a goldfish and persuaded the Doctors to give it to Peter, promising them a full show of Joy in return. Their agreement wasn't without a future barb. Mattison cleverly saw the fish as something to give and then take away, over and over again, perpetuating shows of delight and of grief.

The Viewing plan was to keep Peter in his bedroom, place the fishbowl on the playroom table, and then send the child in alone. Dainig was to signal at the first sound of Peter's awkward footsteps, so the audience could watch him discover the fish and savor every moment of his reaction.

Dainig's earphones were already alive. He heard Cooper say, "Go along and play now, boy," and caught Peter's obedient answer, followed by the tap of his feet. He arrowed his hand down in the signal, and fastened his eyes on the "melting" wall. This was one Viewing he intended to witness full-out.

Abruptly, Peter was there before him, headed in his perpetual path to the toybox. The fishbowl rested on the table where he couldn't possibly overlook it, the carp glinting in spurts and darts of lacey fin and sun-gold body. Dainig held his breath, waiting for the boy to notice . . . and then Peter did!

Halfway to the toys, he stopped dead, turned full around, and stared at the thing on the table. In a hushed moment of still-life, the sight registered in his slow brain, then his face broke apart in recognition and he thrust out his hands, shouting, "My fish! You came back! My fish!"

He stretched out his arms and rushed to the table where he fell to his knees and touched the bowl with a two-handed caress—gently—his nose against the glass as he peered at the bit of gold in the water. "You came back to me," he cooed in a strange, baby voice. "I love you! I miss you!"

When he couldn't contain the joy, he scrambled to his feet and jumped up and down, laughing and hollering, "You aren't dead, are you? Mama and Daddy aren't dead, are they? They're only lost, too. I love you, Fish. We can be together now, and . . ."

He broke off, expression jumping from his face, the delight jolted into a bewildered stare that shot right out through the invisible wall.

"Who—who—?" he whispered, backing away. Then he darted for the fishbowl and circled it in his arms, sheltering it defensively while he stared at the wall as though it were threatening him.

Something was wrong! The boy was terrified! Dainig jerked off his headset and dashed headlong out of the auditorium and through the hall to the door in Peter's bath. When he reached the playroom, the crisis was explained in one glance.

The yellow wall was transparent from Peter's side, too! And the rising rows of the audience were visible as faces lined up like ominous blobs with eyes peering out of them.

"Clear the auditorium!" Dainig shouted. "There's been a power failure!" He knelt and clutched Peter, trying to turn him away from the sight.

The people outside wouldn't move! Ordered, and even

prodded, they only edged away, and Peter wouldn't stop watching them, all the while protecting his fish.

"Get out of the auditorium," Dainig screamed. *"He can see you!* Hurry!"

The anxiety inside him almost equaled a drug-emotion as he felt Peter tremble in his arms. He had to take command! Peter must not be allowed to witness any more of this.

He scooped the boy up, fishbowl and all, and rushed him into the bedroom where he continued to hold him, confused and shaking, his face as blank as the rest of humanity's.

Then Cooper and Mattison were there. Cooper barged on into the playroom to berate the technicians, demanding immediate restoration of the wall, and threatening dismissal right and left.

When Mattison moved, it was to the little bag she had brought with her. She took out a hypo-gun and aimed it at Peter's trembling arm. "A sedative," she said, as the drug stung its way through the child's skin. "Let me get the fishbowl away from him before he drops it and makes a mess."

Her efforts were fruitless as Peter clung to the bowl with the strength that surprised Dainig. But his fingers slowly grew lax, and Mattison lifted the bowl away.

"Put him on the bed," she ordered Dainig. "He's too heavy to hold."

Dainig obeyed. But if Peter had been heavy, he hadn't noticed. He laid him down, his white-blond head on the pillow, and sat beside him, letting the boy cling until he even gave that up and fell into a near-sleep.

"Doctor Cooper?" Mattison called. "What is the situation?"

Cooper came in, red-faced from shouting, but emotionless. "Under control. The wall is back to normal. There are going to be a lot of changes in personnel around here."

Dainig heard it all, but kept on staring at Peter's sleeping face, wondering what the boy had felt when his world suddenly opened into a nightmare? He had *seen* what Peter experienced spread all across his face, and sensed it in the shaking of Peter's body. But, how had it actually "*felt?*"

Mattison broke his thoughts. "Stay with the boy until he wakes up, Dainig. He won't sleep long. It is up to you to think of a way to get his mind off this so he will forget it by this afternoon's Viewing. I don't care what you tell him—just do it."

"He won't forget *this* that fast, Dr. Mattison. It was too traumatic. He'll never be ready by this afternoon."

She met him with her cold eyes. "If you prove to be right, we will forego the last two Viewings for today. But he has to begin again tomorrow. Is that understood?"

"Yes, Doctor. I'll do everything I can."

An hour later, Peter roused. His eyes flared, and he bolted straight up in the bed, disoriented.

"Peter!" Dainig said sharply. "I'm here! Everything's all right." He wasn't sure how to calm the boy's agitation, since he couldn't feel it for himself.

Peter slithered out of the far side of the bed and raced for the playroom. "*Where are they?* Where is the window?"

"There *is* no window, Peter. You can see for yourself."

"Yes, there is! My fish came back and so did my window. I want to see out, Danny." He searched along the yellow wall. "Show me!"

"You've been asleep and you had a bad dream, Peter."

"No! I saw people. Just like I see from my window."

"*Saw* from your window," Dainig corrected for the hundredth time. "You don't have a window, anymore. Now, calm down, Peter. I don't want you all excited."

"I can't help it. The people are right outside, and maybe my Mama and Daddy are there, too!"

"Your mother and father are dead. I've told you that before. You understand what 'dead' means. You had a goldfish, and one morning it was dead. Remember?"

"It came *back*. My Mama and Daddy are out there, Danny, and I've got to look for them. I've got to see the street and find my Mama and Daddy. Matty won't do it, and they're worried about me."

"They're dead, Peter. They can't worry about anything."

"They always worry." Peter faced him, trying belligerent threats. "You show me, Danny, or I'll cry!" His eyes were already full of tears.

"Not now," Dainig said feebly.

"I will! And I'll never stop. I don't like this place, anymore. I'll cry and I'll never stop. You'll see."

"Don't threaten me, Peter. No one can cry forever."

The boy went back to pleading. "Please, Danny! My Mama is . . ."

Sense and logic couldn't reach him. He was obsessed with this idea and, like the mental baby he was, would hold onto it until it faded out of his unretentive brain. Dainig used everything he could muster, but nothing helped. When he realized that *he* was now searching for a nonexistent window, he gave up.

He told Peter, "I'm going to get your lunch. I don't want to hear another word about this, do you understand? When I come back, I expect you to be playing quietly, like a good boy. Then, you'll eat. I'll see you in a little while."

He left Peter still searching the wall. The only allies he had were Time and Peter's feeble brain.

But when he returned, Peter was even more upset. He roamed the floor, pleaded and cried, and adamantly refused to eat. Dainig took the untouched tray with him to Cooper and Mattison to punctuate his demand that the rest of the day's Viewings be cancelled. For once, they let him have his way. Tomorrow would be soon enough.

This time, tomorrow never came. Peter refused his food, dissolving into a mass of tears and beggings, and it required an injection to make him sleep through the night. Dainig stayed by his bed, hoping for the boy's sake that the morning would bring a change.

It didn't. But the Viewings went off on schedule, because this burst of emotion was a bonanza in Mattison's opinion. Dainig endured his time in the auditorium with his back turned to Peter's wall, concentrating on the audience with malice. They quivered—drinking deep of Peter's hysteria—and he built a notion that they watched the child in a state of near-desperation, all at once aware that they were witnessing a living human treasure in Peter and his soul-cries. Dainig didn't understand them any more than he understood himself and his grating thoughts that shouted, *"Is this right?"*

As far back as the turn of the century, it had become apparent that human beings with normal emotions could not survive the superfast pace of change and overcrowding. Neurosis and nervous breakdown were commonplace in everyone over the age of twenty-five. When it grew patently obvious that the only two alternatives left to modern society were nervous collapse or total apathy, the government scientists had moved swiftly, instigating Anti-Emotion Conditioning. If people couldn't survive with emotions, then emotions must be erased.

"Then, why retain even a vestige of a useless, evil thing in the crippled intellect of a child like Peter?" Dainig questioned. "To keep a link with our Past," the textbooks said. "Emotion is an inborn human quality. Since we are human, we must not forget what emotions are."

Today, Dainig doubted those quotations, and saw Peter's purpose with new insight. Perhaps a dangerous insight. A crippled child was used because people were afraid to risk a fully emotional adult. In other words, people were afraid of *themselves*, as they were naturally born.

Dainig suddenly understood why the "watchers" left the Viewings so full of a sense of accomplishment. In spite of the necessity of AEC, they somehow sensed that they were only half-alive. They *needed* Peter. Since they couldn't "feel," themselves, they needed to see *him* "feel."

So, Dainig stood in the auditorium and peered meanly into their faces, investigating the new insight in his own desperate need to fill his mind with sense. His extra hours in the boy's company were getting the best of him. The effect of Peter's thundering emotion was so overwhelming that, even when the child was sedated, Dainig still heard his cries of, "I have to find my Mama and Daddy! Open the curtains. Let me see the street!"

The Doctors were obsessed, too—but with pride. These performances were stirring the world to comment. As yet another day swept by, the only part of Peter's state to rankle them was his refusal to eat.

Dainig stayed with Peter around the clock, seeing his body grow thinner and his eyes swell shut from crying. His throaty screams were hoarse, ugly sounds.

On the fourth day, Mattison threatened force-feeding. Dainig couldn't face helping with it, but had to agree, because he had no control over Peter. The child was now a frenzied "creature," exhaustion gaining on him. Perhaps, Dainig thought, even Death.

All the while, the public received its emotional voyeurism in overflowing doses. They saw Peter clawing against the wall, his hands reaching—pressing—scraping—as he searched for the window he couldn't find, his face contorted with dry sobs that didn't produce tears, anymore.

Dainig was down to his last idea, and unauthorized or not, followed through with it, positive that Peter would die without release from the hysteria.

He caught the child close in unyielding arms and told him the whole truth about the Viewings, shouting to slam it in over the cries. His *own* Fear was a tangible presence in the room as he talked on and on, waiting for Peter's reaction.

Blessedly, Peter started to quiet, and eventually slipped to the floor where he huddled deathly still, mulling over what he had heard. The new silence of him was overpowering.

He stayed that way for many minutes, but just as Dainig dared to be hopeful, a radically new idea roared out of the boy. He demanded to be let OUT! Not to have the window back, but to be *released* so he could search for his parents and be *with* the people on the street.

There was no restraining him. The new tack was worse than the old, since it added a wider dimension. Peter flew with it. Dainig sat down, totally spent, and let the child's frenzy buffet him in the torrent he knew would *never* end, now.

When the Doctors learned what Dainig had done, they called him in and pelted him with accusations of insubordination, stupidity, and even insinuations of personal deviation. He slumped before them too defeated to worry about what they said, numb from the bombardment of emotions he couldn't experience, but still sensed as actual forces beating on him.

"I had to try," he said weakly. "He's going to die of this if something drastic isn't done. You two haven't succeeded, either."

They met each other's eyes silently, then Cooper responded, "I suppose you're right in that much. But, you're adding up a shaky score, young man. From the look of you, I think you know it."

"Are you ill?" Mattison asked, her voice flat.

"Only from continuous anxiety. I'm experiencing it full force. But . . ." he added quickly, ". . . don't ask me to let someone else take over. Peter needs me. It he's going to make it through this at all, he needs *me*."

"I wasn't going to suggest it. Nevertheless, give yourself some relief, Dainig. Take a dose of Euphoria and be happy for a few hours."

Dainig nodded in assent, knowing he wouldn't do it. Fake happiness wasn't going to buy him any relief. Nothing was. He was destined to watch Peter spread-eagled against that yellow wall, pounding on it, shouting it away, until the child's body grew too weak to hold him upright and dropped him at the foot of it.

Along with the mental image, Dainig had a sudden, futile wish that he could "care."

By force of habit, Dainig plodded into the cafeteria on the morning of the fifth day, collected a cup of strong tea and a sweet roll, and sat down at a secluded table. His mood was sour, and he needed time alone. Time to build his courage toward the ordeal of Peter's force-fed breakfast. When he tried to eat his roll, he choked on the first swallow and dumped the whole thing back onto his plate. The dry lump of it in his throat felt too much like a round, rubber tube.

He was slumped in his chair, brooding over the teacup, when a green-Coveralled torso loomed into his vision, and a too-loud voice assaulted him. "I trust this is a *second* breakfast, friend."

Cursing silently, Dainig straightened to acknowledge

Richmond. "It's the only one, as a matter of fact. I can't face anything more."

"That's quite obvious." Richmond sat down, taking his welcome for granted. "You look worse than you did the other day. Didn't you ever shake that down mood?"

"To hell with the down mood, Rich! Can't you understand that I'm exhausted? Change places with me for a day and you'll know why."

"Edgy, too, I see," Richmond shook his head. "You're talking about Peter, of course. Well, you don't have anything to fret about on that score, friend. He's giving some great performances."

"Sure—from your side of the screen. I see a different picture, and I see it all the time, so if you don't mind, I'd rather not spend my one free hour discussing it."

"Sorry." Richmond wasn't sincere. "I think I know what you mean. What we're getting isn't normal Crying. It's Hysteria, right? And you look like you've been through it all the way *with* him. I labeled you gray the other day. Now, I'd call you Black! Is the pounding wearing on you?"

"I can look after myself." Dainig took a sip of his too-hot tea to keep from speaking the words that bit his tongue. He was overly sensitive today—too aware of tonalities—so he had to be careful. Richmond had an insinuating edge on his voice, and Dainig didn't want to probe it. "You're mistaking exhaustion for depression. Anxiety can be brought on by both, you know. You picked the wrong cause."

"I say 'No' to that, friend. You've been dogging around under this mood far too long." As he spoke the next words, his tone changed to a clinical iciness which stole their innocence. "Be honest, Dainig. Is Peter's state, added to what you were already carrying, putting you off-balance?"

"No!" Dainig's answer was too loud. It turned the other

heads in the room. He continued more softly, "Although I can't think why it doesn't. That child is going to die if we can't pull him out of this, and no one else seems capable of understanding that fact. No one else knows him the way I do—his stamina—his . . ."

"I'm aware of your special position. But none of it should touch you enough to cause this erratic behavior. What's the *real* problem, friend? Your depression is starting to worry me. Are you positive that you're not . . . ?"

"Not what?" Dainig glanced up quickly. "Finish your sentence."

"Forget it," Rich subsided. "Just be sure you search out the reason."

"There's no search necessary. It's exhaustion, plain and simple. Nerves."

"No chance that it's Peter, himself? After all, he hammers away with no relief. That could put the crunch on anybody, and when it comes to *you* . . . ! What is your Sensitivity Score, anyway, Dainig?"

Dainig shuddered. And the reaction scared him doubly because he couldn't account for it. Somehow, Richmond had touched fire from his low-burning anxiety. "I'm a Two. Why?"

"Aren't you actually closer to a One?"

"You don't tell a friend that he's in a non-drug depression and then ask him a question like that! I'm not going into Reemergence, if that's what you're trying to say."

"Easy. I'm not attacking you," Richmond soothed. "I only ask because I have some knowledge of the subject. If you notice symptoms, they're easier to straighten out when they first appear. Too many people stall around until they're *forced* into Reconditioning. The full, hard way."

Dainig was pinned on one word. Reconditioning. The physical pain and public disgrace of it was a terror that lurked in those who came out of AEC with a low Sensitivity Score. One day, through trauma, through an unexpected assault on their nervous system, they might again develop emotions and be imprisoned in the dark cells to have those "feelings" wrenched out of them by force of agony. He was pinned on the word, but refused to flutter against it, because it wasn't true of him. *His* "ghost" was unnamed. It wasn't called Reemergence.

He wanted no more to do with Richmond. The man was totally insensitive, a machete hacking him away piece by piece. He snorted, "You and your Reconditioning! You're entering the work, so you're suddenly hunting down candidates." He faced the man, taking the offensive. "What is all of this, Richmond? Are you trying to undermine me? To edge me out and take over my job with Peter? You can't get it, you know. You were turned down before. Not enough Insight, I think the report said."

"All right!" Richmond's pride was smarting. "But if *your* brain is as sharp as your tongue, why don't you show sense enough to swallow a dose of Euphoria and get yourself above this thing?"

"I don't have time for games like that. I can't be on drugs when I'm with Peter. Especially not now!"

"Then, you intend to suffer through in this terrible state of mind?"

"Do you really care?" Dainig challenged. "You know you don't. You're incapable of it."

"And—*glad* of the fact."

Dainig didn't acknowledge the knifing innuendo. He simply stood up. "I'm due back with Peter."

Surprisingly, Richmond took to his feet, too. His hand came out and pressed hard into Dainig's arm. "Take my warning and do something about your depression, friend. It could be a sign of trouble. And—I've *seen* the Labs.

I don't want to walk in and find your name on one of the cells some day. For God's sake, man, stay out of that place!"

Dainig met his blue eyes, aware that his own were stark.

The initial force-feeding was accomplished. Thankfully, Dainig wasn't commanded to hold Peter down. Straps served that function, and a medical doctor did the work with the help of two nurses. Under orders, Dainig remained outside so his presence wouldn't get mixed in Peter's mind with the gruesome procedure. He stood in the hallway and clenched his fists against his ears to stifle the screams and the gagging. When the medical team filed out, he watched them go with sickness in his soul.

None of this was going to save Peter. No one could force enough nourishment down him to sustain his life, when the hysteria, like the crush of prolonged pain, was eroding his strength to nothing.

He went in to Peter and offered his physical presence, but turned himself off to the rabid flailing at the wall, as he sifted through his own crisis-thoughts. Peter's fate wasn't actually of much importance to the world, and he had to face that fact. There was a six-year-old retarded girl already waiting to take his place in an Old World AEC Center. It would hurt Cooper and Mattison to have the limelight shift from them, but it would be a hurt of pride, not of remorse.

Everyone else was weathering this trial as stoically as always, but for some reason, Peter's torture was translating itself into a menacing knot in Dainig. If Peter died, Dainig's job would be gone. Mattison and Cooper were high enough in the echelons to be secure, but Dainig's work would be forfeit. A man naturally feared a threat of that kind.

His only remedy was to take action. To *do* something.

Peter's fit had to be broken. The child must have a rest—a breather; time to calm himself and come back to normal living. That was imperative. With his motive clear, now—his own livelihood, which meant his future—Dainig vowed to supply Peter's needs.

He shuddered through the remainder of the day. It brought three Viewings and a second force-feeding which Peter vomited twenty minutes later. Then, in the predawn hours of the next morning, he made his move. Leaving the boy unattended, he managed a secret trip home, went out to an all-night store, and sneaked his way back again.

The corridor was murky. Only a few base lights glowed as he crept along, carrying a small brown case close to his body. He took care to move silently when he entered Peter's Complex, but caution wasn't necessary. The boy still tossed in his drugged sleep, restless against the medication, but unconscious.

Dainig stood still in the soft light and looked down at Peter's ravaged face, sensing himself as a granite man staring at pure vulnerability. When he realized the granite was cracking, he shook himself loose. Picking up the knife and fork from his own supper tray—which he had deliberately neglected to return to the kitchen—he walked into the playroom. Everything he did in the next minutes must appear "possible." It wasn't going to be easy, but the result was worth any effort demanded of him.

The yellow wall was a fragile thing. If attacked properly, it could be broken. There was never any danger of such an attack, since nothing heavy or sharp was left in the Complex where Peter might hurt himself with it. Tonight, something *had* been left: the utensils on his supper tray, and a pointed metal pole from a children's game which Dainig had brought on the pretext of trying to interest the boy in something new.

Using those three flimsy weapons, he attacked the wall at a height Peter could have reached by himself. He scraped and jabbed, not worried that it took a fair amount of strength. Peter's frenzy had already proved that it gave him abnormal bursts of power.

In ten minutes time, he had clawed out the first jagged hole. From that point on, it was easy. He ripped at it with his fingers, then rammed the table against it, making it bigger and bigger, reminding himself that it only had to be a large enough squeezing-space for a small, thin body.

When the size suited him, he wriggled through it feet first and crawled out into the auditorium. Groping in the dark, he opened the hallway door, left it standing ajar, and ran down the corridor to do the same with the street door, thanking heaven that they always opened from the inside, locked or not. He returned through Peter's bathroom, wanting no reentrance marks on the sides of the hole to give him away.

In the dim light, he bent over Peter and removed the damp, sweaty pajamas, careful not to disturb him enough to rouse him. Next, he opened the brown case and dressed the child in a Coverall he had purchased—blue, and cut in the fancier fashion of a girl.

The brown case was now empty, except for the final, most necessary thing. The wig. It was dark brown, and long—a girl's hairstyle. Dainig placed it on Peter's head, holding the boy still with one strong arm. When he straightened up, he was trembling.

Fear had become a familiar thing to him, so he let it run. Thrusting his forearms under Peter's prone body, he whispered, "Come on, little boy. You're not going to die from the very quality that makes you so treasured. Danny's here. Just be quiet."

Peter stirred, but didn't wake with the gentle handling,

and Dainig lifted him into his arms. He grappled up the case and carried the boy out through the bathroom door, closing it securely behind him.

He took Peter to the apartment of one of his present sex-partners—Tina Halper—naturally having the key. She had chosen this particular time to take her vacation away from the city, and her choice was more important than she had imagined. With the child tucked safely into her bed, Dainig spent the rest of the night pacing the floor, denying himself the release offered by the vial of Euphoria tablets huddling in Tina's cupboard. It was crucial that he keep a close watch.

With sunrise, Peter started to awaken, and Dainig administered another dose of sedative to keep the boy asleep until there was time to spend explaining things and introducing him to his new surroundings. Peter could make good use of the added rest, anyway. There would be no Viewings for him to perform, today.

Dainig left for the Center early, expecting to sound the alarm and invent fast excuses for his absence during the night. But there was already a crowd around the building, and when he shoved through it, claiming priority, he found the Center's halls teeming with people who should have been at thier desks. They all had two statements blurting out of their mouths at sight of him: "Peter's gone;" and, "Cooper wants you in Peter's Complex *immediately!*"

Cooper had been there before him, then. Gulping back a new burst of Fear, he made the dash, setting disbelief on his face for everyone to see. When he entered Peter's rooms, he pretended a thorough inspection of the broken wall, stalling the curses he was sure would lash at him from Cooper. But Cooper only touched his arm and led him silently to his own office where Dr. Mattison waited.

When the door closed them in together, the two of them began to talk over the top of Dainig as thought he wasn't even present.

"This is totally impossible," Cooper stated flatly. He would have been angry, if he'd been able to feel anger. "The boy was sedated."

"Dainig reported that he was restless for the last few nights, in spite of the drug," Mattison said.

"Very restless," Dainig thrust himself in to underline the important point. "I was always afraid he was going to wake up and begin screaming again."

"And you weren't with him last night, apparently." Cooper said it as a point of information, not a question.

"No, sir. He hadn't managed to shake off the sedative before, so I took your advice and spent the night with a Euphoria-drug. To try to relax."

"Looking at you, I can't see that it did much good," Mattison said.

"Not in light of *this*!" Dainig methodically followed his preplanned way. "He must have been completely wild to break through that wall. And—I have to take the blame. I was in such a hurry to get to the happy-drug that I left my supper tray behind. That must be what he used. My knife."

"*And* the pole-toy you gave him. It was by the hole, too," Cooper said.

"So, it's my fault from start to finish," Dainig admitted. "But—where can he be? He's bound to be terrified outside. He's never *been* outside. Why hasn't someone spotted him? Everyone knows his face!"

"Calm yourself," Mattison told him. "There is a general search in progress, and he'll be found. He can't have gone far. Although, who knows when he escaped."

Dainig stood up, determined. "I'll go out and hunt, too."

"That's foolishness."

"But, I caused it! Out of selfishness. Out of trying to feel a few hours of fake happiness while he was going through the deepest pits of . . ."

"Enough!" Mattison commanded. "At any other time, I would agree, but looking at you . . . You're a shambles, Dainig. Your appearance is nearly as deteriorated as Peter's. We'll leave the summing-up until after he is found. The blame has to be placed, but there were more factors in this situation than your stupidities of last night."

Dainig turned away, pretending humility and gratitude for her understanding. He meant neither one. He had counted on her cold, efficient mind to see all sides of the matter. "What do you want me to do, then?" he murmured. "I don't have any work here except Peter, but I could help coordinate the search."

"Go home," Cooper ordered. "Sleep. You're not needed until Peter is back, so you'd best use the time to pull yourself into some semblance of shape."

"I don't think I have the right to rest."

"You do as you are told, Dainig," Mattison spoke sharply. "When you have earned your own authority, *then* you can use it."

"Whatever you say, Doctor Mattison. And—maybe I can take some comfort from the fact that I did sound a warning. I told you this emotional spasm wasn't like the others. That this one wasn't something Peter was going to forget and put behind him. Still, I never . . ."

When Peter showed the barest sign of awakening, Dainig roused him deliberately. He wanted some of the sedative left in the boy's system when he opened his eyes to the new apartment, so he could listen to the explanation with some quantity of calm. He told Peter the whole story, holding fast to his hand in case the truth was too frightening for him. Peter accepted it without a second's doubt. He could see for himself that the bedroom was different, and he had no strength to make a fuss, anyway.

When Dainig finished, Peter pointed to the side wall. "Is that really a window, then? Do you mean that?"

"I do."

"Will all those people be outside it? Looking at me like you said?"

"No. This is a real window—like you had when you lived with your Mama and Daddy."

"And no one can look at me? And Matty and Coop can't be mean to me?" Suddenly, his arms were around Dainig's neck in a tight hug. "You let me out, Danny! I love you for letting me out."

"Thank you, Peter." Dainig returned the hug as he had learned to do, by acting it out.

"Can I open the curtains so I can see?"

"It's afternoon outside, and the light would hurt your eyes. I want to put cold towels on them for a while and relieve the swelling. You've been crying for so long that . . ."

"*Please* let me look," Peter interrupted. "To be sure the faces aren't there. Please!"

Dainig had to give in. "All right, but just for a minute. You look at the street while I get the towels. Then I want you to rest, and eat some soup, and rest some more. You have plenty of time, Peter. All the time you need to recover. I only ask that you do exactly as I say, so I can *give* you that time."

With evening, and two bowls of vitamin-loaded broth inside Peter, Dainig administered another injection of sedative and put him to bed. He didn't like to leave him alone, but there was no choice. Peter needed several days to completely shake off the hysteria and be manageable. Until that time, Dainig had to be partially available at his own apartment to intercept calls from the Center.

He preset the apartment's communicator to link with his own home number, and taught Peter how to press the one button necessary to reach him in an emergency. That was all he could do for the present. As he left, he wished that the door weren't operated by a panic lock that could always be opened from the inside. But he trusted Peter, certain he would never try to open it. The boy was satisfied with the window, and had never in his life opened a door for himself.

One day passed. Peter gazed out the window in fascinated silence, gaining strength as he lived in a state of emotional balance with no forced ups and downs. He was simply "happy." Dainig saw it, and envied it.

"You *do* have a special power," Daining told him over lunch on the third day. "You've gone from despair to contentment so fast it's unbelievable. Maybe resilience is part of being able to 'feel.' It's an interesting thought, anyway."

"Yes," Peter agreed, without understanding a word Dainig had said. "I'm special. I know it, now. I have my window and the street back, and all I need is my fish. Where did it go this time?"

"I'll get you another goldfish. But, you must understand that it isn't the same one you had before. You have to get it through your head what 'dead' means."

"I know what it means. It means that something goes away for a while and then comes back again. Nothing ever stays away. Not my window or the street or my fish or my Mama and Daddy. Pretty soon we have to go out and look for them."

"No."

Peter's mouth formed a quick pout. "I'll cry."

"Oh, no, you won't. I'm not going through that again."

"You just wait and see."

"Turn it off, Peter. I don't intend to watch it."

"Then, say we can go out and look. I want to be with the people. I don't like it all alone."

"We'll see," Dainig half-surrendered, because childish mind or not, Peter was pushing him into a corner with his threats. The boy's strength wasn't up to another emotional attack. If he worked himself into one, he would die *here* just as readily as he would have died at the Center.

Dainig filled the next two days with frequent, lying trips to Cooper's office, with cooking for Peter, and fighting off the boy's incessant demands to go onto the street and be with people. Peter hadn't yet come to tears, because Dainig's returned threats held him in check, but it wouldn't hold off forever.

The boy gained a half pound, but Dainig didn't. Anxiety ate up all of his calories as he delayed the inevitable time when he must return Peter and face whatever his own punishment might be. He kept on delaying it because something was happening in the outside world that put him off-balance, and spotlighted him as more of a public enemy than he had intended to be. People were clamoring for Peter with a totally unexpected reaction.

Lethargy had settled over the city—even the world. The same people who had watched Peter's performances out of fascination suddenly lost that fascination, and exhibited the odd things Dainig had recently noticed at the Viewings. They missed him. They wanted him. They valued him as a precious object.

The news media put it dramatically. *"The human heart is absent from the world." "With Peter gone, Humanity is gone."*

Without one emotional human being left within their sight, they thought *no* human beings were left. That if *no one* could love, laugh and cry, yearn, giggle and despair, then human wasn't Human, and spirit and soul were lost, too.

Dainig understood. He wasn't cut off from the pestering, chameleon Peter, but he appreciated the people's loss. They accepted Anti-Emotion Conditioning as necessary to survival—as a fact of life—but deep within themselves they had tallied the cost and found it too great. As he had, at times, himself.

This reaction had never occurred before. People normally abided the few days famine between the destruction of one Viewing Child and the initiation of another. But, Peter was *lost*, and this held some special significance, some mysterious human meaning.

Even Peter noticed it. Looking out the window, he said, "The people seem funny, Danny. They walk different. Like they're tired."

"Everyone has his own problems. Don't worry about it."

"But it *is* true, like you said. Not one of them ever laughs. Do you know that? And you never laugh, either. Aren't you *ever* happy, Danny?"

Dainig only stared at him blankly. How could he answer?

"I wish you'd laugh with me, sometimes. When we wrestle or play games, it would be more fun if you laughed, too."

"You don't know how right you are," Dainig thought. Yet he had nothing to laugh with, and no reason to do it, anyway. The relief the prospect offered was too much to resist, so even fully aware of its sham, he downed a dose of Euphoria and spent that morning being happy with Peter. Strangely, it was a "happier" happy. Peter's spontaneity made it almost real.

By noon, Dainig's drug and Peter's natural joy had both worn off, and the boy *insisted* on being taken to the street.

He talked about it all through lunch, and his threats changed into brief outbursts he couldn't control. "I *have* to go out," he begged. "My Mama and Daddy are *lost* out there."

"Peter!"

"Well—all right, then, they're dead and they aren't lost. But I still have to go out and be with the people, Danny. Please. I never am. I never saw the street up close, or heard the noise."

Dainig put down his fork and stared at the boy, trying to get inside his foggy brain with some simple truths. "You're not being fair to me, Peter. I took a terrible chance when I brought you here. I was trying to let you recover. I never intended to take you out on the street. This is only a short visit so you can get well. Do you understand?"

"Yes," Peter answered, his expression downfallen. He actually did understand this time. "But . . ."

"There are no 'buts.' I could lose my job over what I've done. I'm hoping Matty and Coop will forgive me when they see how much better you are, but if I go too far . . . they might send me away. And I couldn't be with you, anymore. Ever."

Peter grabbed his hand, frightened. "I want you to stay with me! I'll be *all* alone if you don't. But—Danny!" His eyes were wild with confusion. "Oh—help me! I don't know what to do! I want you, and I want the street, too. Just one time, Danny? I won't ever be able to do it again. What can I do?"

Peter was caught in his own trap. As his body trembled and tears started in his eyes, Dainig sagged. No matter what he did for the child, it always led to a bigger decision, to a larger crisis. If Peter worked himself into another frenzy . . .

"Danny?" Peter asked in a high, quaking voice. "If I don't go now, I never can. Matty will put me back where people can look at me, and then I can't ever be on the street. *You* can go on the street. Why can't I ever?" He added desperately, "I love you, Danny."

Dainig shook his head to clear it to some sense, but it wouldn't clear. Everything Peter said was true. Once back in the Complex, he would never see daylight again. Everything had gotten out of hand, anyway. Dainig's job was sure to be forfeit, no matter *what* else he did. "You have a way of . . ." He gave up, slapping his hand against the table. "You picked the right man to wheedle. I'll take you out, if you promise to do everything I tell you."

Peter raced around the table and threw his whole body onto him in an exuberant embrace. "I promise! I'm a good boy, and I promise!"

"And, *I'm* the Moron," Dainig muttered. "But you have the right to see the world at least once." He added, to himself, "*Although you'll detest it, when you find out it's not fine and wonderful.*"

Using makeup he found in the dressing-table drawer, he darkened Peter's face and hands from their normal translucent fragility to a healthy beige-brown, put the little girl's wig on his head, instructed him to hold tightly to his hand, and took him out.

The first blast of street noise sent Peter up against him, shaking. Yet, he refused to return to the building. As they walked slowly, surrounded by people, jostled, bumped, and swirled around, Dainig tried to see the street as Peter must be seeing it.

First would be the noise from the voices and the roaring Commuters that carried passengers from one end of the giant city to the other, augmented by the Air-Commuters zooming overhead. The rest would be coming to Peter in a blur: Color—churning and bouncing on clothing and painted signs; bodies—swarming clutches of them, that pushed at him and knocked him about until he practically walked on top of Dainig's feet to keep from being stepped on; conversations—jumbled together until none of them were intelligible; and the overwhelming presence of faces, faces, faces—or, from Peter's lower vantage point—legs, legs, and feet.

Peter clung to him, but kept on walking, showing astonishing bravery. His small, hot hand asked for something, but Dainig didn't know what it was, or how to give it. Was Peter asking for comfort? How did a man give comfort? He couldn't "feel," so he was unable to give "feeling." All he could do was stand straight and strong and hope it was enough.

After ten minutes, he led Peter back, wary of facing him with too much shock. When they entered the apartment, he looked down into the boy's overlarge eyes, and said, "It wasn't such a wonderful place, after all, was it?"

"I don't know yet," Peter answered. "I was afraid at first, but it started to go away. I don't know yet. I think I can like it very much."

Dainig was the one to register shock.

As he pulled the wig off Peter's head and washed the boy's hands and face, he finally reasoned it out. With his dull brain, Peter probably *wouldn't* experience the strangling sensation of the crowds and the noise. Maybe a man could keep his emotions and survive in this society, after all. *If* he had low-level intelligence.

He left Peter watching TV, which was now concerned mostly with stories about his own disappearance, and checked in with Dr. Cooper. The news there wasn't good. He had missed three calls from the Center that morning, and was informed that they weren't the first to go unanswered. Cooper was curious as to where he had been, but his curiosity was nothing compared to the glint of suspicion that flashed in Mattison's eyes. His excuse—that

he'd been out hunting for Peter like everybody else—
sounded lame.

Riding an Air-Commuter back to Peter, his anxiety
mounted higher and higher, but he consciously determined
not to let it change his mind. Peter was going to have one
more day free of his cage, and that was that. It was odd
that he now thought of the Complex as a cage, but he did.

On a lucky hunch, he spent that evening at his own apartment, so he was there when Mattison appeared at his door.
She pushed inside, investigating the empty rooms without
an invitation. Although she found nothing, he was uncomfortably certain when she left that her suspicion wasn't
dampened.

Morning broke with a heaviness that, if he'd been able to
"feel," he would have named Dread. It was Peter's last
day. It meant seeing him locked away, and then facing the
Doctors with the truth. He put the thoughts down. This
was Peter's morning, and his own problems weren't going
to spoil it.

Peter was awake and ensconced in front of the TV when
Dainig returned to him. "Why aren't you looking at the
street?" Dainig asked. "The curtain is open."

"Because. I can see people here, too—in the TV window.
Only—it's not much fun." He faced Dainig, a question
spread all over his face. "Am I being a bad boy, Danny? I
mean—if all the people are sad because they can't find me,
like that man in the TV says, then I'm being bad, aren't
I?"

"You are not. Those people can't feel sad, anyway. They
can't feel anything."

"Are you sure?"

"Of course. Now, come and get washed for breakfast. I
saved an egg for you. How do you like that?"

"And then can we go on the street again, so I can hear the noise?"

"Why not?" Dainig had said it before he considered, but now he asked himself, "*Why not?*" He couldn't make things any worse than they already were.

Peter cocked his head slyly. "I weebled you again, didn't I?"

"You what?"

"I weebled you."

Dainig hesitated, trying to translate. The meaning finally came through as Peter's mishmash of the word "wheedled." "Yes, you did," Dainig chuckled deep in his throat. "You're the best weebler I ever saw."

Peter was staring at him round-eyed, his face blank.

"What's wrong?" Dainig asked quickly.

"You *laughed*, Danny," Peter whispered, drawing the words out as though they were a miraculous secret. As Dainig's eyes flared, he added, "I won't tell on you. You can even laugh again, and I won't tell."

Suddenly, the child's babbling didn't strike Dainig as innocent. He put a fast end to it by going to gather up the little-girl disguise.

They went onto the street again, with Peter dressed as a girl, and this time it took only five minutes of clinging before he was walking a foot away from Dainig, enjoying the sights. Dainig wished there were a way to erase the wonder and happiness from the child's face. Someone was bound to notice. No one else displayed such expressions past the age of five.

People were moving more slowly than usual, their eyes raking the crowds and down the spaces between buildings, stupidly hunting for Peter in places that had been investigated hundreds of times. Dainig hung onto the boy's hand tightly, aware that he was the possessor of what everyone now considered to be the last Human Being in the world.

As they passed a dim walkway between two eighty-story towers, a voice called, "Pee-terrr! Pee-terrr!" It came from an old man who shuffled along, stopping beside every deep window-well to peer down into it.

Peter pulled up short, then started for the man. Dainig jerked him back.

"But, Danny! That man is calling for Peter," the boy complained. "*I'm* Peter."

"Sshhh," Dainig silenced him. "Never say your name on the street. Never! Now, remember that."

"Yes, Danny. But I should answer when someone calls me. You always say so."

"Except for right now. Just keep on walking. We can't dawdle. Enjoy yourself, while you can."

They had been out for an hour when a Commuter stopped nearby, and Dainig recognized one of the men who stepped off. Richmond! The man should have been busy at the Center! He clenched his hand onto Peter's and strode faster. If Richmond saw him—and the small figure beside him . . . !

Peter stumbled with the fast pace, but Dainig pulled him along anyway, desperate to put the crowd between them and Richmond. Just as they reached another walkway between buildings, a shout blared out from behind him. "Dainig! Hey—*Dainig!*"

Dainig's legs screamed to break and run, but he held himself in check and turned around to judge the situation. Richmond was a good distance behind, so Peter's shortness must certainly be hiding him from view.

"Dainig!" Richmond yelled again, and Dainig spotted the man's head craning to see over the crowd.

With one swift motion, Dainig lifted Peter off his feet and rushed him a short distance down the walkway. He plunked him down, and whispered firmly, "Stay right here and don't move until I come back for you. Now—*mind me!*"

He raced back to the street and pushed through the crowd to intercept Richmond twenty feet from Peter's hiding place. "I *thought* I recognized your voice, Rich." He continued with his lies. "Are you searching, too? It's a futile process, but compulsive."

He exchanged news and anxieties with Richmond for three eternity-strung minutes, his mind on Peter, frantic to find out if the boy was staying put. He finally managed to send Richmond off in the opposite direction, and shoved his path back to the walkway.

His stomach nearly jumped out of his body when he saw what was happening. Peter was exactly where he had left him—but he wasn't alone! An old woman was bending over him, and they were talking.

As he neared, he heard her say, ". . . and that's why I'm looking so hard to find Peter. I'm anxious about him. I can't even eat when I think of him being lost and alone. Or, that I might never see him again."

"But, you mustn't worry," Peter answered her. "You mustn't be sad. It's not nice to feel sad. You might cry, and I don't want you to cry."

"I might *cry*?" The old woman straightened up. "You talk very strangely for a girl your age."

Dainig stepped in quickly. "Yes. She does—right now." He circled Peter with one arm. "She's just coming out of a Depressant-drug, so she sounds odd. Please forgive her."

The old woman peered straight into his eyes and shook her head. "A drug for a child that young. It's gone so far, hasn't it? No one can *ever* replace Peter. We have to find him, or we can't even pretend to be human, anymore."

She shambled off in her continued vain search, her legs scrawny and slightly bowed inside the Coverall pants, her pale, bleary eyes hunting in areas where there wasn't even a chance of a hiding place. "Poor, *poor* old woman," Dainig murmured, then jerked up, wondering why those words had sprung into his mind.

Whatever the reason, he had no time for it. He took hold of Peter and hurried him back to the apartment, with the sensation of watching eyes following their progress all the way.

Peter was exhilarated from the experience, and once inside, he jumped around the room in uncontained joy. "I love it here, Danny! I love everything there is about it. It makes me so *happy!* I don't think I'll ever cry again. Thank you, Danny. Thank you for bringing me. We'll stay here all the time and go on the street, and I'll have a fish, and . . ."

"You'll have your lunch," Dainig said gruffly. He couldn't help the gruffness. This outing had proved to be too much. It had shown him two things he didn't want to see: Peter's joy at being free, and humanity's unfelt, but real grief over his loss. When he returned Peter to his "cage," humanity would have what it wanted. But at what expense? The peace and joy of a forever-child.

He left Peter to the TV and went to the kitchen. Facts had to be faced. And, now. He had to search them out, weigh them, and come up with the right balance, impossible as that seemed in his present state of mind. The imagined sight of leading Peter back into the Complex blinded him. He would never be able to do it. Maybe he couldn't "feel," but something inside him was *screaming!*

That was where the whole decision became unbalanced, because the thought of returning Peter shouldn't be affecting him at all. The truth that it did, pointed to a terror-filled fault in himself. He stood there with the uncracked egg trembling in his hand, and admitted it.

"I am beginning to FEEL! God help me, I AM!"

His menacing Sensitivity Score had proved inescapable,

and he was going into Reemergence. He hadn't really been worried about his own future livelihood at all. He had been harboring and growing an affection for Peter!

"It's all because of him," he told himself. "No one could withstand him." But, excuses wouldn't change the fact. He was beginning to "feel," to "care;" therefore, he was a Deviant in society. There was only one solution for such Deviants. Reconditioning. Just as Richmond had warned. Reconditioning, with all of its agony, shock, and social stigma.

The moment his aberration was discovered, they would manhandle him into a dark brainwashing cell, give him to a stony-faced Reconditioner, snare him with sensor electrodes, and pit him against paroxysms of sonic and electric pain, until his soul was washed clean of illegal emotions.

He cracked the egg—shattering the shell as *he* was shattering.

There must be a way around it! He could take Peter back, make Mattison and Cooper see that he had saved the boy's life by his action, and at the same time, afforded them a longer period in the world spotlight. If he hid his aberration well enough, he might get off with no more than dismissal as Peter's Companion, and expulsion from the Center's classrooms.

It meant living as a Deviant for the rest of his life, but if what was starting to awaken in him *was* emotion, he knew he could exist without too great a hardship. "Feeling" wasn't as uncomfortable as he'd been taught to believe. And once named, his "ghost" wasn't so formidable. All he had to do was take Peter back. . . .

He slammed a fork into the egg and whipped it yellow. The idea of imprisoning Peter was still unthinkable! His condition of dawning emotion made it doubly repulsive. He *cared*, now. Only a little—but he did care. Coming to a balanced decision was impossible when the scales had three sides.

He fought to clear away the fogginess of the new-born emotion and make use of the methods he had employed all of his life: Logic; his belief in human rights; and conscience—in the sense of justice for a fellow human being. The process of doing it calmed him, and inevitably led in only one direction. When he found that direction, it opened light into his mind—a way out for both of them—for Peter, *and* for himself.

He grasped it firmly and made a solemn vow. Peter *wouldn't* be forced back into that cage to be abused for the amusement of people who were incapable of experiencing the tiniest twinge of what they demanded from him. He *wouldn't* have to cry on cue, anymore. If he was normally unhappy, all right—but he would never be tortured into tears.

It followed with easy logic that if Peter wasn't going to have to do these things, Peter had to disappear. That meant that Dainig had to disappear, too, taking Peter with him.

It was obvious, but it also stacked up a mountain he couldn't climb. To move about in society required an identity number and a card, both of them direct links to the Population-Control Computer. They would be tracked down in no time.

With so much urgency pushing at his brain, it flashed to answers. The one he finally chose demanded a terrible risk. As a student in Anti-Emotion Conditioning, he was allowed access to the Computer's programming section. If he really meant his vow, he could take advantage of that access to enter a false number for himself, leaving Frederic Dainig on record, but unused, and then fabricate a background for Peter. If he dared, *both* of them could escape their prescribed futures!

He set the final plate on the table and straightened, trembling. It hinged on whether or not he believed in his vow to save the boy. He had that answer even as he called Peter to come and eat. He believed in it with his entire soul.

He let his breath out, realizing that if he were practiced in the art of emotion, he would be smiling.

Peter wasn't smiling. He came to the table, subdued.

"Where did your happiness go in such a hurry?" Dainig asked him.

"I was watching the TV window. The people are still sad, Danny. They're still hunting for me."

"They won't find you."

"Then, they'll stay sad. And cry? I won't want that lady to cry. My Mama never cried. Only me."

"*You* won't be crying from now on, either. I've decided things for us, Peter. You don't have to go back to Coop and Matty. You and I will stay out in the world forever."

Peter's mouth fell open in astonishment. "Really? Truly? And I'll have a fish?"

"You'll have *two* fishes. One must get lonely all by itself. You can even have three! What do you think of that?" An upward muscular spasm had hold of Dainig's mouth. Alien as it was, he accepted it and labeled it, surely. A spontaneous, natural smile.

"Gold ones?" Peter built on his excitement, jigging up and down. "And orange ones? White? And . . . ?"

"Yellow and black and polka-dotted. Whatever is to be found." Dainig's entire body seemed warm and light.

"But, mostly I'll have *you*, Danny. And Coop and Matty won't come. Will they? To hurt me?"

Dainig willingly relinquished his smile to say intently, "Never again. I'll watch out for you, Peter. I'll be there for you—whenever you need me—all the rest of your life." He reached out and stroked the boy's pale hair, silky and warm under his palm.

"I love you, Danny."

"I know! Isn't that wonderful, Peter? I actually *do* *know*! And—and—*I* love *you*, little boy."

Peter stopped deathly still. "You never said that to me before. Not once."

"I've never *felt* it before, Peter. Everything has changed. You and I are alike, now. I can feel things, too."

With one leap, Peter was in his arms. Whether or not he actually understood it, he realized that Dainig's transformation was miraculous and important. Between his laughs, he shouted, "Then, laugh with me, Danny! Be happy with me!"

Dainig consciously tried, but it came weakly. Something stood in the way.

"That wasn't very good," Peter complained, hugging him harder.

"For heaven's sake, give me time to learn. To practice." The frail body felt different in his arms. For once, it fit: comforting and comforted.

Dainig absorbed the tumble of new feelings gratefully. It appeared that once emotions started to reemerge, they came like geysers, erupting harder and faster, with swifter and swifter frequency. He had swept from an overreactive Fear, to a chuckle, to brief Pity for an old woman, to Love —in the space of a few days. What was next? Waiting to find out was going to be difficult. His worries would be heightened, too, but that prospect cancelled out to nothing beside what he was experiencing right now.

He welcomed every twinge of "feeling" with an open body: heart, stomach, blood, and breath. He was soaring! Alive with bubbles! Emotion was pure freedom, and he was never going to let himself be chained again.

"Oh, Danny! This will be better than I ever thought anything could be. You make me so happy all the time!" Abruptly, and with no warning, Peter's arms were off of

Dainig and the boy stood back, stricken. "But—all the people will still be sad."

Dainig sighed. "I don't even want you to think about that. Eat your lunch, little boy. I'll worry about the people."

Extracting Peter's promise to be good, Daining left the apartment and caught a Commuter to the building which housed the giant Computer. He was sweating when he entered, and sweating harder when he came out. But it was done.

He now carried two identity numbers for himself: one for Frederic Dainig, and another for a nonexistent man named Daniel Weber. Nestled with them was one for a boy named Peter Weber. That one would seldom be used. He intended to hide Peter as much as possible, letting him into the world only when he could walk with him and protect him, shielding the nature of his dull mind. But, if it should be needed, the record of Peter Weber was duly complete and registered. They would live in another city, and Frederic Dainig would simply vanish from this one.

He felt the stir of non-drug happiness touch his skin from the inside out, and relished it. Not even the fear of what he was doing, nor the immense problems the future would bring as his responsibilities with Peter grew, were so terrible. Not when he had moments of elation like this to balance them.

The elevator doors opened onto the apartment's floor, and Dainig stopped dead. Peter was in the hall—coming toward him!

"What are you doing outside the room?" Dainig shouted. *"You don't have the wig . . . !"*

He heaved Peter into his arms and fled inside the apartment where he plunked him down roughly, almost making him fall. "You promised to mind me! You promised! What did you think you were doing?"

Startled, Peter became defiant. "I knew you wouldn't let me, so I had to!"

"Had to *what*, Peter?"

"Go back alone. And you let me do it, Danny! You *let* me. I'm not bad. I can't make people cry, so you let me do it!"

Peter was standing away from him, cowering. Dainig realized the boy was afraid of his shouting. He walked to the center of the room and lowered his voice to a calm tone. "Let's talk about this, Peter. You have to explain it to me, because I don't understand what you mean. Now —come here. Be calm, and come here and tell me."

Peter edged closer, then closed the distance and threw his arms around Dainig's waist. "You made me afraid, Danny," he cried. "Don't be mad at me and leave me alone. I *have* to do it. Help me!"

Dainig knelt down to the boy's level and held him just far enough away so he could see his face. "I'm not mad, Peter. I only want you to explain. *What* do you have to do?"

"I have to go back where they can find me. I don't know the way by myself, but I have to be where they can watch me—so they won't cry."

"You don't *ever* have to go back there, Peter. I've arranged it so . . ."

"No!" Peter wasn't really hearing him. "I want to. I'm being a bad boy to hide. I feel so sorry when I see the people ready to cry. It's not fair to have everybody crying."

"They are not capable of crying! Now, look—you can't possibly understand what going back to Coop and Matty will mean for you, but I do, so you have to trust me. Coop and Matty will find another child to take your place, Peter.

But if you go back, you'll always be there. You'll keep on crying over a fish, or your window, until the day comes when you finally comprehend that you're being tricked into it. That day *will come*, Peter, and when it does, you'll be . . ." The rest of the sentence dried to sand in his mouth.

"I'll be let out?"

Peter was seeing hope where there was none, so Dainig was forced to say it. "No. When that day comes, Peter, you will be—dead."

As usual, the boy didn't respond to the word. "Dead," to him, meant going away for a while and then reappearing. He said, "Maybe I'll come back to this place after I'm dead. Or maybe even back to my own window."

Dainig shook his head in frustration. The child *had* to understand. His cooperation was essential to their combined safety. "Peter, now listen to me carefully. If you go back to Coop and Matty, you will *never* get away from them again. You will be there for the rest of your life."

Peter's face darkened. "Always?" he whispered. "But, I don't want to do that. Please, Danny . . .!"

"You don't have to do it. You don't! I've fixed it so you and I can stay together in this big world, and you can have a real window, and all the fishes you want, and me to love you—for the rest of your life. It's all settled."

Peter's dread flashed away, and he leaped into his highest gear of delight. "That's wonderful! *You're* wonderful, Danny! I love you!" He hopped around the room, his arms flung wide, the joy bubbling even in his feet. "Never go back—never go back—never go back. . . ."

"Not so loud," Dainig warned, shaken by the exuberance. "We have to stay quiet until we're out of here. I'll get what clothes I have in the closet, and we'll leave right away. I've picked a nice big city for us to live in, Peter, where no one will ever find us."

As he said the words, he felt "lighter." Peter's freedom

had become tangled in his own, and his terror of Reconditioning would vanish along with Peter's torment.

"I'll get that funny hair you put on me," Peter ran for the bedroom. He stopped in mid-stride. "No. If we're really going away, then I have to look out the window again. For the last time. You get the hair, Danny." He was immediately at the window, craning down at the street, and engrossed with what he saw.

Dainig gathered up the few remnants of his life he was going to take with him, and shoved them into the familiar brown case. The course was set, and the sooner he started along it, the better.

Carrying the case, makeup, and wig, he returned to the living room and let his voice express his excitement. "All right, Peter, my boy. It's time to make you into a little girl again." Eagerness was new to him, and he savored the leaping of it.

Peter was still at the window, silhouetted against the glare. When he turned, his movement was slow. He came to Dainig almost unwillingly, then stood docilely, waiting for the makeup.

Dainig opened the tube, but his hands were stayed by the gleam of fresh tears on Peter's cheeks: silent tears that dribbled down and fell mutely off his chin.

"What is it?" Dainig asked softly.

"I . . . I don't know."

"Have you forgotten our plans, already?" Dainig kept his voice pitched low, oddly in awe of these tears, sensing something profound in them. "Don't you want to go away with me, Peter?"

"Oh, yes! I want to with all my heart," Peter answered. But the tears still fell. "Only—I don't understand. Can you explain it to me?"

"Tell me, and I'll try."

"I was watching the people on the street and . . . Why

can they make me feel so sad, when everything is wonderful and I'm so happy? I want to cry all the time I'm looking at them. I can't stand to see them sad like that. It hurts me, Danny. Why does it?"

Dainig was silent, and as he stared into the reddened eyes, an unknown "something" pushed him slowly to his knees in front of the child. He reached out and grasped the thin shoulders gently.

"I see, Peter. I wish I didn't, but I do. I learned the word for what you're feeling in one of my classes. It was once called 'Compassion,' and it was considered a good emotion. Maybe one of the best. It means feeling another person's unhappiness, and doing it with love and understanding. It means knowing what another person is suffering, and suffering with him. I think you've just learned a new emotion."

"Then, if I learned it, I guess I'll always feel it, won't I? Even when I'm happy with you, I'll know the people are sad because they don't have me to watch. But—I can't help it, Danny. I *have* to go with you, and stay away from Coop and Matty so they can't be mean to me. I want to be happy, too. We'll be fine, won't we? And, you'll love me?"

A sensation akin to feeling his life's blood ebb from his head and arms to form a pressure in his chest washed over Dainig. He unaccountably found his hands pulling Peter forward to enfold and press against himself. "I just now learned Compassion, too, Peter," he whispered. "Only— I'm feeling it for *you*. I need to protect you—to . . ." He bent his lips to Peter's soft cheek, and their breaths sighed out in unison. Once.

Then Dainig was on his feet. Frightened!

He turned gruffly to the work at hand. "Let's put this wig on you and get out of here, boy. There's no time to waste. None!"

He dressed Peter quickly, detesting the full return of the

child's joyful anticipation of their future together. Because there wasn't going to *be* any future. Dainig was back in his right mind and knew that, now.

All there was going to be was one more sojourn on the street, which he wouldn't even condescend to prolong. Then Peter would be safely back at the Center. After that would come the facing of Cooper and Mattison, the admission of guilt, the repentence, and—surrendering himself for Reconditioning. He would lose his position and his proposed career, but he doubted if anyone would press criminal charges. The agony of Reconditioning would be enough to satisfy even Mattison's sly heart.

For himself, he would face the process staunchly, as he might face a friend willing to relieve him of a fatal, devouring disease. Because, in that moment with Peter—in that one moment on his knees with the child's body clutched close against his own—he had finally felt EMOTION. Full, true, Emotion. And if that tearing, engulfing, throbbing sensation of body and soul was what emotion demanded of a human being, he could never live with it. It was a blight that had no place in human reality.

Leaving the brown case in the middle of the floor, Dainig took Peter's eager hand and led him innocently out of the apartment. When he closed the door behind them, he brought his fingers up to his own face and brushed aside the last, and only, tear he ever wanted to shed, then put the remains of it on his tongue and swallowed it, bitter salt and all.

NIZE KITTY

by Alan E. Nourse

TELL ME, FRIEND—do you happen to own a cat? No, I don't mean do you like cats, or do you keep a cat, or do you have a cat around the house. Sure you do. Lots of people do. My wife found one somewhere a couple of months ago and brought it home, and it turned out to be the most pregnant damned cat that ever conned a free meal. She named it "Queenie" and got very defensive about its delicate condition, so it looks like we're going to have a houseful of little princes and princesses in a few more days.

Well, that's my problem and I'm stuck with it—but if you think *you* own a cat, that's yours. Take a tip, friend: you don't. I know, you keep one around, you feed it, it sleeps on your feet at night, and rubs against your legs and purrs and purrs, and everything is cozy. That's nice. I envy your innocence. Everything was cozy for me, too, until I spent a day on the job down in the Graveyard last week and found out a thing or two about cats. Now I am out of a job, I have a nine-thousand-dollar gyro-car to pay for, I am the current Big Joke of the Philadelphia Police Force, and the only reason they're not giving me shock treatments is because the shrinks don't think it's worth spending money on the current. My wife is calling me a butcher and threatening to leave, and next week I'll be wiping the noses of a dozen nize little kitties which I could cheerfully drown, but very emphatically won't. The only way I'm ahead is that I know one thing that most people don't: neither you, nor I, nor anybody else owns any cat.

The cat may own *you*. I never did get *that* completely straight, and I'm still fuzzy on a couple of critical points along the way. No doubt someday soon the scholars and politicians and diplomats will get the details all straightened out. But I got the main message, and from where I sit I can't see that the details matter too much one way or the other.

Everything was going along fine until late last week when Murphy, who runs Special Assignments, called me in and said, "Mike, I've got a new job for you. You're gonna love it. You're gonna be the envy of the Department when they hear about this new job I've got for you."

"Great," I said. "What kind of a job? I'm still on that larceny case with Rogers."

"Forget the larceny case. I've got a new job that fits you like a glove. I'm putting you on the Graveyard shift."

I stared at him for a minute. "Aw, come on. You haven't run a Graveyard patrol since way back in '92. What's there to patrol?"

"Oh, it's not a patrol, exactly. There's been a complaint. Specific. Some people on the fringes have been screaming, and when *they* call the cops something is mighty wrong."

"Like what?" I asked him.

"Like noises all night long down there. Loud noises. A regular tub-thumping, according to the complaint. And flickering lights, and strange voices . . ."

I scowled and threw myself down in the chair, disgusted. "Maybe the rats are having band concerts," I said. "Look, Murph—there's nothing down in the Graveyard but a million rats and half a million flea-bitten alley cats. You know that. What are you trying to sell me?"

Murphy shook his head and touched a match to his dead cigar. "I don't know what's going on down there, but I think we'd better find out. Go talk to the people that are complaining. Spend a day or two down there and see what you can see. And if you meet a cat walking down the street pounding a bass drum, take a picture for me. That one I'd like to see."

I started out from Center City Philly in a little Volta two-wheeler with the gyro in the rear, a special Service model with all the protection options. I just couldn't understand Murphy. Nobody ever went down into the Graveyard any more. There wasn't any point to it. The Graveyard in Philly was just about the same as the one in Chicago, or Brooklyn, or New Orleans, or Seattle, except maybe bigger and deader. I guess they got an earlier start in Philly. The buildings were built more than a hundred and fifty years ago—fairly decent houses and factories then, I guess. But by the 1920s they were beginning to fall apart from disrepair, and by the '40s they were slums—whole big chunks up north of Vine Street and west of Broad. In the '60s and '70s people were trying a thousand different schemes to clear them out and put up new buildings, but it costs money to clear out twenty miles of rotting real estate with a quarter of a million people living there. And then, with the freeways, people began moving out. The ones that couldn't make it to the suburbs made it to the fringes and left the center to rot. By the late 1980s there was nothing left in the middle but buildings nobody would repair, and nobody could sell, and nobody could afford to tear down. No plumbing, no power, no nothing. The buildings began to collapse of their own weight. The sewers caved in; the water pipes rusted; the pavement began to buckle. What weather and termites didn't take care of, fires did. Nobody lived there any more. Nobody ever went there. The cats and the rats had it all to themselves.

We called it the Graveyard, and I didn't like the idea of patrolling it. I wasn't sure why—it's the people on the fringe that make the rough duty—but the idea of going into the middle was spooky. There probably hadn't been a Police two-wheeler bounce through there in ten years, and I was a little bit queasy about being the first.

I drove down through the fringe streets along the river first, with a list of complaint calls to check out. Finally I found the address given by one of the complainers. I'd be complaining, too, if I lived there; the Graveyard is spreading out into the fringes just as fast as people move farther out. Even here there were only a few buildings still occupied and it looked like they never pulled up the blinds. I pounded on a door that threatened to give at the hinges with every blow, and pretty soon a fat lady with a baby under one arm opened the door a crack and said, "We don't want none," and slammed the door again.

I pounded some more. This time she threw the door open and glared at me. Then she saw the squad car down on the street and slammed the door again even harder.

Finally the gentleman of the house appeared. He was short and ugly, with a dirty undershirt and three days of stubble on his chin. "OK, piggie, what's the beef?"

"You tell me," I said. "You're the one calling the cops. Something about some noise?"

"Oh, yeah," he said, calming down a little. "A man can't get no sleep nights, with all the racket over there."

"What kind of racket?"

"Like a thousand kids kicking garbage cans. On and off, on and off, all night long. Just when it gets quiet and you think they're through for the night, it starts all over again." He shook his head unhappily. "Man can't get no sleep with that going on."

"Now, look," I said patiently. "Are you telling me there are people out there in the Graveyard raising Cain every night?"

"Not people," he said. "Cats. Those goddam cats are holding mass meetings or something. That's what I told the pig on the telephone, and he told me I should see a doctor."

"Cats," I said. "You mean the kind with four legs and a tail?"

"Cats," he said.

"Holding mass meetings," I said.

"That's right."

"Tell me, mister, have you actually been over there to look?"

"Well—I went in a little way."

"You've seen one of these meetings, hah?"

"Not me! Don't catch me going in *that* far. Ain't good for a man . . ."

I'd forgotten how superstitious some of these fringers were about the Graveyard. "How do you know it's cats, then?"

"I know, that's all. That old warehouse there . . ." He pointed across the piles of decaying buildings to a long brick affair half a mile in. "Go see for yourself, wise guy. But you'd better watch your step." He rubbed a couple of long scratches on his forearm, and glared at me. "They won't like you poking around."

"The cats," I said.

"The cats."

I was the wise guy, all right. I thought he was crazy!

The Volta didn't do so well once I got past the first few blocks. Half the streets had caved through into the sewers; the others looked like they were ready to. Roofs had fallen in. Walls had collapsed. The streets were knee-deep in rubble—rotting wood, bricks, old rags, discarded junk. And the rats were everywere. The rats depended on the fringers for food, of course, and lived mostly in the outer edge of the Graveyard, but they were smart enough to know that nobody would come exterminating them here, so here they nested. And then there were the cats. I've lived in Philly for over twenty years now, ever since Sally and I got fed up with Brooklyn back in '83 and decided to try a change of town. Since the first day I was here I've tripped over cats. They are the meanest looking bunch of cats I've ever seen anywhere, any time. The ones I remembered from the old days of Graveyard patrols weren't any different, except bigger, but even they used to turn and slink away when they heard a gyro humming down the street.

They say a Volta with a gyro will go anywhere but straight up a brick wall, but they hadn't figured on streets like these. By the time I was within a block of the warehouse that Undershirt had pointed out, that car was whining like an overloaded crane. I stopped on a level chunk of cobblestone, put the car on park, and slid into a pair of lead-rubber hip boots. Then I checked my stun-gun for pellets. The boots would keep off the rats; I figured the gun could handle anything bigger that might drift my way.

Even with that I was nervous. You hear lots of stories about people going into the Graveyard and never coming out. Silly, of course, the kind of thing mothers tell their kids to scare them away from here, but still, stun-guns had been known to jam at the wrong time.

The warehouse was half gone. The north wall had fallen

in, and so had the roof. There was a deep crevice through the floor where the foundations of adjoining houses had shifted years before. The place was empty and looked like it had been abandoned for centuries. I poked around a few minutes, and scared an alley cat out of a packing case. He snarled at me, and slid off into the rubble. No threat there, I thought; and I didn't see anything that looked like any mass meeting to me.

But this was where the man had said the noise was coming from, so I snooped some more. There was an office cubicle at the other end of the warehouse. The door fell off in my hand as I tried to open it. Inside was a ramshackle desk, a fairly good window facing out on the alley with all the glass broken, and a set of filing cases.

For lack of anything else to do, I started on the filing cases. The drawers weren't locked, but they were stuck. After working up a sweat I still couldn't open them. I looked around, and found an old tire iron to use for a jimmy.

Just as I was set to pry open the first drawer, a voice behind me said, "Doc, you're wasting your time."

I swung around fast. There was nobody there but the cat I'd scared out of the packing cases. He was a huge yellow tom, and he was a beat-up cat if I ever saw one. One ear was hanging in tatters; the other was slit right down the middle. His tail looked as if it had been gnawed off about halfway down. He sat there and looked at me with the nastiest big yellow eyes you ever saw.

I stared at him, and then peered around the room. I don't usually just hear voices. When I hear them, somebody is there. But now the room was empty. I looked at the cat, and then shrugged and started on the file again. I just got the tire iron in place for a good try when the cat said, "I'm telling you, stupid, you won't find anything in there."

This time it *had* to be the cat; I was looking right at him. And the voice *sounded* like a cat—a sort of high-pitched, hissing voice that prickled my scalp. Either that cat was sitting there talking to me, or the old brain had suddenly started missing.

The second alternative shook me up, all right, but I liked it better than the first.

"Look, Doc, why don't you just go on back home and mind your own business?" the cat said.

"Now wait a minute!" I howled.

"What's wrong?" said the cat.

"Cat's can't talk," I snapped back.

"Yeah?" the cat said. "I can talk you into the ground any day, if you want to make a contest of it."

I just stared at him, shaking my head. Deep down, I knew there was no way that cat could be talking to me—but all of a sudden I had a powerful urge to be doing something simple and basic and exceedingly down-to-earth. There was nothing I really expected to find in those filing cases, but right then I turned my back on the cat and started tugging on the file drawer like it held the crown jewels. I got my foot up on the case for leverage, and I heaved away at that drawer for dear life. Then it gave with a crash, dumping me on the floor and scattering useless old invoices all over the room.

"Now look at yourself," the cat said in a disgusted tone. "All because I tried to give you a little helpful advice. Look, you people go dog-wild for your scientific method, right? So use it. What makes you think cats can't talk?"

"They just can't," I said, dusting myself off and rubbing my leg.

"Who says they can't?" said Tom.

I fought for a grip on myself. "Nobody ever heard a cat talk before."

"So? Does that necessarily prove that they can't?"

"Well," I said stubbornly, "if they can, then why don't they?"

"Why should they?" returned the cat, looking immensely pleased with himself. "Give me one good reason."

I sat down on the desk. I felt as thought the floor were sliding out from under me. "I . . . I . . . well, maybe just to be sociable," I said lamely.

The cat made an obscene noise. "Sociable! Huh! It's tough enough living with you humans as it is, without having to be sociable too." He licked his whiskers and settled back with a toothy yawn.

Something in my mind was kicking like a balky mule. "You mean to sit there and tell me that any old cat can talk if it wants to?" I asked.

Tom looked at me sadly. "You know, you people just don't have any imagination at all, do you? You don't see something happening all the time, so you just assume it can't happen. Just because we don't waste all our time and energy jabbering like you do, you figure that we can't. Well, why should we? *You* talk enough, and what good does it do you? Ninety percent is just words to fill in embarrassing silences, and the other ten percent doesn't mean much. You still build cities you can't live in and hold jobs you don't like and keep right on scrapping and bickering and figuring out new ways to annihilate yourselves." He flipped his chopped-off tail, and settled down with a sigh of self-approval. "Why don't you get smart, Doc? Like us."

It wasn't what he said so much as that damned supercilious way he said it. As thought there just couldn't possibly be anything quite so perfect as "us." "What's so red-hot about you?" I snapped.

"We use our heads."

"I haven't noticed anything so smart about cats," I said with some heat.

The cat shrugged. "Well—we've been taking you people for a ride for the last five thousand years, haven't we?"

"Oh, now look here . . ."

"We haven't cared for it too much," the cat broke in, "but it's been better than nothing. It isn't pleasant being mauled and slobbered over and baby-talked to—but then, we've had it pretty soft. And you give us a good laugh every now and then. Here you are, always knocking yourselves out, working like mad to stay in one place, scared witless of practically everything including your own shadows, building up your silly governments and chopping each other to ribbons. And all we've had to do was keep our mouths shut and we've been in clover ever since you crawled out of your caves. Strictly clover." He grinned at me and began licking his paw. "It's a shame to lead anybody around by the nose, I guess, but if you've been stupid enough to sit still and take it all these years, why blame us? We can't complain. We get fed. We get taken care of. We get protection. If you hadn't gone softheaded for those nasty dogs of yours, things would have been one hundred percent cozy —but the dogs don't worry us too much, either. They're almost as stupid as you are."

I suddenly realized that this insolent hunk of fur was getting to me. "I suppose you clever cats have yourselves organized into some kind of worldwide society to keep us from discovering you," I said, as scarcastically as I could manage. "A secret Master Civilization, or something."

"Not a chance," said the cat. "Civilization is for suckers. Why be civilized? You're doing all the work, and we're getting the pork chops. Every cat for himself, I always say, and the less I see of the others—*get out of here, you chiseler, he's mine!*"

The abrupt change of voice jolted me, but the change in Tom shook me even more. Suddenly he was on his feet, ears back, fur out straight, hissing ferociously. Then I saw why. Another cat had come in, a huge ugly calico, with a sneaky-looking gray Persian behind him. The Persian got one look at Tom and backed out again with a snarl, but the calico squared off, arching his back and spreading his claws and making nasty sounds in his throat.

Tom moved like lightning. With one great leap he was on the calico, snarling and clawing, and the two cats dissolved into a howling, whirling bundle of fur. I jumped aside as they came spinning across the floor like two fighting furies. Then suddenly, Tom was decisively on top, clawing like a demon, and the calico went leaping and twisting across the room under him with an awful yowl. Finally his contortions threw Tom off; with a final vicious swipe of his claws the calico turned and went caterwauling through the door like a multicolored streak.

Tom did everything but dust off his paws in satisfaction. "Teach him to cut in on *my* territory," he snarled, hopping back up on the windowsill and stroking back his ruffled fur. "Civilization, pah! There are plenty of other humans around . . ."

"And it's every cat for himself, you say," I said nervously.

"You better believe it." The cat paused for a moment, considering. "Except in emergencies, of course."

"Emergencies?"

"When it looks like you humans are getting out of hand," said the cat. "Then we *have* to get together. Like now. There are probably a quarter of a million of us meeting here every night now, quite a crowd if I do say so . . ."

"You mean quite a cat fight."

"Well, sometimes. We have an awful time keeping order —everybody trying to sound off his own ideas at once. But it's pretty obvious right now that *something* has to be done to get you people back in the rut again. Before you wipe *everything* out."

"You mean with bombs?"

"And smog and poison and filth and all the tricky little gadgets you think you're going to use on each other."

I plowed through the implications of that one, and then started laughing. "And a convention of *cats* is going to stop us?"

"You just wait, Doc." There was an ominous glitter in his big yellow eyes. "You've got about a month left, give or take a few days. You folks have needed a good straightening-out for a long, long time, the way we see it. Now you're going to get it."

I was very glad, right then, that nobody was standing there watching me. Here I was, talking to this cat the way I'd talk to Jack O'Casey over a beer, and getting hotter by the minute. I didn't like that cat's attitude one bit. I've seen people that were too smug to tolerate—and they had insecurity complexes compared to this big yellow tom that sat grinning at me from the windowsill and licking his paws. "I suppose," I said, "that you and your friends are just going to take things over?"

"You might put it that way," he grinned.

"And what will this—uh—'taking over' involve?"

"The works," said the cat. "We've been letting you go along thinking you really ran things for yourselves and just kept us happy out of the bigness of your hearts. Now we'll have you run things just strictly for us for a while." He nodded slowly. "You won't have time to worry about anything else," he added.

I laughed. "How do you think you're going to accomplish this little feat?" I said. "You have some kind of super-weapon, maybe?"

"We have claws," said the cat, very smugly. "We can scratch. Also, we know that a few billion stupid humans won't believe it until it's all over. Are you keeping a cat at home? Just try touching a hair on its head. *He* might not stop you—but your wife would."

"It happens to be a she," I sighed. But Tom was right. Sally was pretty fond of that little tramp she'd picked up. "So you can scratch," I said. "How does that get us in line?"

"Friend, when a cat drops on your back and starts letting you have it, you stop what you're doing, right then. You don't do anything else until you get rid of that cat, and I don't care what you're in the midst of. You stop."

"And if *that's* your secret weapon, why are you telling *me* all about it?"

"Just to see you squirm," Tom said nastily. "You won't be able to *do* anything about it. Once we start in on you, you won't have time."

He sounded so *sincere*. I burst out laughing. "I never heard anything so wild in all my life," I gasped between hoo-ha's. "So you're going to scratch us till we behave, huh? Why, we could wipe out every cat in the Northern Hemisphere in three hours flat. We could obliterate you."

The cat gave me an odd look. "Just like that, eh?"

"Just like that."

He regarded me for a moment, then yawned as though he had suddenly lost interest in the proceedings. Then he closed his eyes. It took me a minute to realize that he'd gone to sleep. "Hey!" I yelled. "Stopped you on that one, didn't I?"

Tom opened one eye and sniffed. "Are you still here?"

"You'll have to admit we could do it."

"Doc, if that's what you want to think, be my guest. It doesn't bother *me* any."

"Well, how could you stop us?"

"From, uh, 'obliterating' us?"

"From just wiping you out."

He looked at me. "You know, for a bunch of clods you humans have had a couple of brilliant flashes from time to time, you just never had the imagination to see what they meant. Take the blackies, for instance. You humans don't like black cats too much—you never have. But has anybody ever stopped to think just why a black cat should mean bad luck? Never! And then this business about cats having nine lives. You've almost tumbled there for a thousand years, but you never quite made it." He shook his head from side to side. "You're so *dense*. Why *nine* lives? Why not seventeen? Or a hundred and thirty-seven? Why, you people couldn't kill a cat if you tried for twenty years."

That was too much. "Puss," I said, I think you're the biggest liar I ever ran into. What's more," I said, "I think maybe I'll just call your bluff." I pulled the stun-gun out of my belt. "See this gadget here, Puss?" I said. "*It kills cats.*"

The cat just yawned. He didn't budge off that windowsill. "You probably can't even hit me," he sneered. "the way your hand is shaking. Why get so excited, Doc?"

I let him have it. I figured I might hate myself later, but a man can take just so much from a cat. I pulled the trigger, and I saw old Tom give a jerk as the protoplasmic shock wave went through him, and that was that. I had one dead cat on the windowsill.

He was dead, all right. He didn't even twitch. I picked him up by that chewed-off tail and dropped him back into the packing case.

Then I took a deep breath, and looked around me. I decided I didn't care about snooping around much farther. I just wanted to get out of that place, fast.

"Well, that's one pellet shot to hell," said a voice at the window. "Want to try again?"

I whirled. It was the same voice—*exactly* the same voice—but a different cat. At least it looked different. This one was black with white-and-tan markings on his face, and a long black tail that kept twitching and twitching. But the eyes were the same—big, yellow, and nasty-looking.

"Thanks, Doc," the cat said. "That was a pretty sad frame to have to go wandering around in. This one's a lot nicer."

"Now wait a minute," I roared. "What are you, anyway?"

"Just exactly what I was five minutes ago. I just converted."

"You converted," I repeated.

"Of course."

"Well, where did you convert from?"

He shook his head. "Wrong question. You want to ask *how* did I convert, or else what did I convert *through?*"

I was shaking all over. "All right, *what did you convert through?*"

"Sorry. Trade secret." He hopped down onto the desk top, and started to rub against my arm, purring like mad. I jumped as if he'd bitten me. "Relax," said the cat. "I'm not going to hurt you. How could I? After all, I'm just a nize little kitty. What could I do?" He started licking his paw. "Damn shame I couldn't have made it all black, though. I've never been all black yet. Those blackies have really got it easy."

"Easy for what?"

"For measuring up a conversion. Miles of range instead of just a few hundred yards. It's a cinch for them, and of course they have a lot wider choice . . ."

"Look," I broke in, almost pleading. "I *shot* that cat. You *can't* be him."

"You want to try it over again?" the cat asked. "Go ahead. Try it as often as you want. You'll get tired before I will. Look, stupid, I've got two hundred and twenty-three possible conversions measured up within easy range, and at least fifteen of them are ripe right now."

"But you can't just keep popping back—the world would be overrun with cats," I protested.

"Oh, when we get old enough we can't convert any more," said the cat. "But until then—you just *try* to kill us if we aren't ready to die!" Suddenly he seemed to be laughing at me. "Why don't you just go home, Doc? I've got a lot of things to get done before we move in on you poor clods."

I stared at that cat, and suddenly I found I was shaking in my boots. It all hit home in a flash, and I suddenly knew I was talking to the same cat I had been talking to before I shot off my stun-gun. And second, I knew that if that was true, then everything else was true, too. If that cat said his pals were getting ready to take over in a month or so, give or take a few days, he wasn't just fooling.

Fighting to hold my hands still, I stuck the stun-gun back in my belt and started backing away toward the door. I didn't quite get the "conversion" business at that point, and I wasn't sure I wanted to. I'd killed a cat that didn't stay dead, and that was enough for me.

The cat did nothing to stop me. He just grinned maliciously. But when I got to the door he said, "Just take a tip, Doc. Don't try to tell anybody about our little talk. Tell them anything else you feel like, but don't tell them the truth." He grinned once more, a big toothy grin. "They'll never believe you."

With a howl I turned and bolted through the door.

I should have taken the cat's tip, but I wasn't smart enough. I was scared silly, and mad enough to scream, and shaking all over when I got out of that building. When I got back to the Volta, I found the street had caved in under its weight and buried it in a heap of rotten concrete. I jumped into the hole, and scraped my way into the cockpit and tried to drive it out anyway, but all I managed to do was burn out one of the gyros completely, which takes some doing. Really shaken now, I climbed back out and half-ran and half-limped out of there, over rubble heaps and rat packs, anything to get out of that Graveyard, and seeing cats behind every trash can. When I reached the fringe I found a call box that was working and called the department and babbled something incoherent about them sending down a wrecker to dig out the car. Then I hung up and looked for a taxi home.

Sally had had dinner ready for two hours when I drifted in, and she was plenty sore. She wasn't any happier when she saw the ripped shirt and the grime all over my best suit trousers. Then that tramp of a cat she'd brought home slunk into the kitchen. With a snarl I snatched up a bread knife and started after it, and Sally went through the roof. She screamed and hung onto my arm until kitty hid under the sofa. "You monster!" she wailed. "Trying to murder a poor helpless kitty . . ."

"Helpless!" I exploded. "You just don't *know*, that's all! I spent the whole damned afternoon talking to one of those 'helpless' cats, and they're about as helpless as barracudas." I waved my arm wildly toward Queenie, sputtering. "They're going to take over, that's what they're going to do, they don't like the way we've been running things so *they're* going to start running things. And you *can't kill them*, I shot that cat right between the eyes with this stun-gun here, and a minute later he was right back there *talking* to me . . ."

Sally edged away from me. "You . . . talked to a cat this afternoon?"

"Look, I know it sounds crazy, Sal, but listen just a minute." I took a deep breath, and then I started telling her about my day, right from the beginning. You should have seen her face. First she looked suspicious, and then puzzled, and then angry, and then she was laughing as though she were going to roll over and die from it.

"Well, what's so funny?" I demanded.

"Oh, you silly. All this because you got some dirt on your trousers," she giggled.

"Dammit, woman, I'm dead serious."

Now there was a real concern on her face. "Mike, you actually *believe* all this?"

"What do you think I'm telling you? It's a big conspiracy! The Graveyard is full of the nasty beasts, and we haven't got much time left, either. The joke is on *us*—can't you see that?"

"Well, it's perfect nonsense," she snapped. "And I don't believe a word of it. You just want to get rid of Queenie before she has her litter, that's all! Well, I think you're horrible! And if you so much as *touch* her . . ."

That was all. We didn't say another word about it. I knew Sally well enough to know that even dropping it cold, she wouldn't soften up for three days, and then she'd need some high-powered coaxing. That should have warned me, even if the cat in the Graveyard hadn't. But Murphy wanted a report. He wanted to know why a nine-thousand-dollar Volta had to be dug out of a caved-in sewer, and what I'd been doing when it fell in. So I told him. And I knew I had to get the message across, fast, to somebody that would listen and help me figure out something to do, too. I rehearsed the story all night long. I knew it would be an uphill climb, so I figured in every con angle I've learned in twenty years of racket work. I told Murphy the tale with enough sincerity to tear the heart out of a corpse.

Murphy heard it from beginning to end, chewing his cigar and watching me. "So these cats are going to take over, hah?" he said.

"In about a month. That's why they're meeting down there, to make plans, and I tell you, we've got to get troops down there or something while we've still got a chance. You can't just kill these cats, they keep coming back alive again! And the worst of it is, I've got this feeling that that cat was telling me something that I wasn't quite catching, something that spells very bad news for the whole lot of us . . ."

Murphy reached for the telephone and said, "Max? Send down a couple of the boys and then get Doc King up here in a hurry. Mike just came uncorked." That was as far as I got with Murphy.

Doc King said I was perfectly rational about everything else, and the three consulting shrinks agreed to "observe" me for a month or so before locking me up. Murphy decided he'd be kind to me, so he fired me on the spot without pressing charges. There wasn't enough left of the Volta to recover, so he sent me a bill for it. And now every time I see the boys from the department they get that grin on their faces and say, "How's your pal down in the Graveyard, Mike?" and laugh out loud when they get past me.

Luckily, Sally has a good job, so we still eat.

As for me, I've got lots of time to read the papers now, and I see that the people in Washington figure the war with Brazil may pick up again any month now, and I see that there are more and more complaints from the fringes about racket down in the Graveyard at night. Sometimes in the past week I've gotten to thinking maybe I *did* slip a cog down there. But other times I know I hadn't. I couldn't shake the growing conviction tapping at the back of my brain that that cat had said and done some things that I just wasn't grasping. Like screaming "He's mine!"—referring to *me*, of course—when that other cat came in. Or like practically daring me to try to kill him, and laughing in my face when I did. I went over that crazy conversation a hundred times in my mind—until finally, last night the answer hit me.

If cats die, and stay dead, we've got no worry from the cats. They can scratch to their hearts' content, and we can exterminate them if they try anything, and that will be that.

But if cats die, and then convert back to life again, we're licked before we start. That was what stopped me. Granted that life is a force or energy manifestation that we don't begin to understand. And granted there might be some sort of metabolic mass-energy transformation that cats know about and we don't. *But the energy has to come from somewhere.* If every cat keeps on living to cat old age, there just wouldn't be enough other cats to convert through. If my bob-tailed confidant could grab some life-energy within range and convert it into a four-footed black frame with white-and-tan spots, and then fit himself into it somehow, he had to get the life-energy somewhere else to start with, and a whale of a lot of it. And that was the trade secret Puss wasn't divulging.

It hit me last night as I sat glaring at the paper, and Queenie came up and rubbed against my leg and purred and purred. Suddenly, I *knew*. That cat didn't like me any more than I liked her. I'd given her no encouragement to come around and get cozy with me. So why should she be purring with such contentment—unless purring didn't mean contentment at all? Unless maybe purring was part of the technique of measuring something up. . . .

I leaped out of that chair and got a room between me and that cat like I'd been charged with lightning. I watched in horror as she came slinking over toward me again, and I was shaking in every bone. All human beings die sometime. When they do, a big chunk of life-energy goes somewhere.

It added up. I knew what cats converted through.

When the time comes, in a couple of weeks or so, the cats will take over, and we can kill them off all we like. They're still going to be here to take over.

I ran upstairs and locked myself in the bedroom, and there I'll stay until Sally gets home to cuddle up to that damned cat. And when Queenie brings forth her newborn in a week or so, I'd give my gold inlays to drown them all. But I don't think I will.

I only wish somebody had tumbled thirty or forty years ago. We might have had a chance then.

THE
KELLY'S
EYE

by Robert Hoskins

THE KELLY HAD MISPLACED his eyepatch again, and in his consequent temper he struck out at Mara, his number-three wife, as she brought his morning beaker. The tribal elders within the chieftan's bedchamber kept their eyes downcast, while those outside visibly flinched as they heard the girl cry out. The signs were not good—Mara had been hard-won just two months ago, and there were still scars of that battle to be seen on the younger men of the camp, those who were not already tissue-hardened by the scars of many years of such battles.

The Kelly cursed in a steady angry growl as he kicked over a bale of tradestuff, bright printed cloth liberated from the caravan chartered by Mara's father. It was better stuff than any the tribe owned, too good to waste on the females, and so it was stored in the Kelly's own tent while he thought on the best use for the pretty.

He glared at the tribal far-seer, empty wrinkled socket gaping red. "Well, old man? Ya ken where it be?"

"No, Captain. I ken not. The darker world is roiled with disturbance. I canna see through the veil."

"Ahhh, what good are ye?"

There was no safe answer to make, although he ducked away from the cuff that would have left his brain reeling, and so the old man kept his own safe counsel. Although in truth it was the Kelly's own fault for losing the thing. If only he would wait for his chambermaid to help him undress at night. The servants-in-waiting knew that they would find the miscreant piece of leather and thong as soon as they were alone to straighten out the tent, but their master had little patience of any sort and none to spare upon reasonable courses of action over small annoyances.

And so the day began badly, with an upset that quickly spread across the entire camp, down to the smallest naked brat plopped into a mud puddle to amuse himself while his mother set about her daily task of being useful to the only man that mattered in her life, the Kelly himself. The undercurrent of almost-fear was felt even by Alan Lenier, as he examined himself one final time before leaving his tent to resume his morning wait upon a barbarian's pleasure. The Kelly's first road of anger had brought Alan out of an unsound sleep to face his third day here on the Trenton highlands.

The man from Yellowknife had followed the trail of the nomads all the way from the Inland Sea. A month ago he had been in Buffalo, the last outpost of the Canadian city-states, spending his supper hours with his fellow junior emissaries from the civilized states to the northwest lamenting their fate at being posted to such godforsaken country rather than São Paulo, or any of the smaller Amazonian principalities. Even the Tasmanian Federation would be preferable to this, although it was half the world away. At least the Tasmanians were civilized.

Buffalo was cramped and dirty and exceedingly provincial, hardly worth calling a city at all. Except for its position astride the Niagara harbor, best port along a thousand miles of the sea, there would have been no reason for its existence. Yet lament its drawbacks though he had, Alan would have been quite pleased to be back there right now, rather than five hundred arduous miles farther south. It was most unfair that fate should have chosen him to be the one to wait thus upon a one-eyed barbarian, begging for his pleasure.

Alan sighed, his romantic nature pleased with the vision of himself as martyr, and even though it was painful to his young heart, his thoughts wandered again to home. The soft summer days would be turning his father's valleyhold into Alan's idea of earthly paradise. Two hours from now the sun that was now steaming the night moisture from the canvas of his tent would break over the blue waters of the Great Slave Lake, and the waters for a dozen miles above Yellowknife would be alive with the bright sails of the sun welcomers. Probably Joab was already out of bed and working by lanternlight over *Redgirl*, to have his brother's boat out at first sunning. Alan had to admit that the boy was already a master at handling the catamaran, far better than ever he had hoped to be.

He passed his hand over his eyes, knowing that idle dreaming was worse than useless. He knew that he could not see Yellowknife and the valleyhold again until this mission was completed, but he could not break himself of the adolescent habit of mooning over the impossible. Why had he been torn from his posting to the Buffalo traders when there were a dozen—a hundred—young men more suited to this sort of wild chase after barbarians. It wasn't at all fair.

Alan knew why. It was his misfortune to be the one to hear and relate the news of a Canadian boy seen in the company of nomads, and it was only logical that the Senate should order him to follow up on the rumor. Perhaps the boy was one of their own, or from one of their close neighbors. It was not at all an unusual thing to have an outpost or a traveling family lose a child to the barbarians—after all, the city-states pursued for the most part an active course of raiding the nomad bloodlines, hoping to strengthen the gene pools. It was only natural that the barbarians would play the game in return, though they were probably unaware of the real reason behind it.

And one of their own or not, the boy should be rescued if possible, ransomed if necessary.

So Alan was here, not in Buffalo, and he could forget about returning to Yellowknife for the summer holiday. Still, it might have been easier on him if this were not his first posting and his first year away from home.

And it might all be for nothing, for there was certainly no sign of a light-skinned boy here. Yet he was certain that this was the tribe —the description of the one-eyed leader was too certain. There were many among the tribes who were maimed of one eye—and more than a few who had been born that way, although most tribes killed a cyclops at birthing—but there were few men who could hold to power with such a maiming. So for three days now Alan had been cooling his heels, joining the sycophants around the tribal fire each morning and each evening.

And as yet the Kelly had not even acknowledged his presence.

Alan checked his golden curls in his field-kit mirror—Sharf at Buffalo had thought that his coloring alone would be enough to win him quick audience with the nomad chieftans. The Nordic strain was rare now, and almost never seen in this part of the world. But the man who told him about the Kelly failed to mention, if he knew, that the nomad's one good eye was an even paler blue than Alan's own, although he had mentioned the hair and beard that were a blaze of pale fire that put Alan's own straw coloring to quiet.

He picked up the polished metal box that contained the gift that he would offer to the Kelly, a beautiful set of antique automatic pistols. The blued metalwork was delicately etched and the ivory grips inlaid, the one gun with silver and the other gold. The box itself could be sealed airtight, and thus was as valuable a gift as the pistols—though the barbarians undoubtedly did not realize its value. But Alan had opened the box too often to make sure that the contents were still safe, and now the silver was showing signs of tarnishing in the salt air. And he had not thought to bring polish to repair the damage.

There were other gifts in his kit, lesser items of lesser beauty and practicality, and he had considered substituting one of them. But whether or not the boy reported was among them, he was sure that this was the tribe he sought. It would take a gift of great value to win the boy's freedom, and so it would have to be the pistols.

He stared at them a moment, feeling an atavistic urge to use them on the barbarian chieftan himself. If it had been Alan's free choice he would have left the camp within an hour of arrival, when he was first told that he could wait with other petitioners upon the Kelly's grant. There were two others at the time, one an old man protesting the demands of the nomad assessors on his orchard, the other a fancied grievance against one of his fellows.

Alan sympathized with the farmer, forced to pay taxes sometimes a dozen times in a year as first one tribe and then another moved down the truncated coast of America, to pause a moment here in the tropic warmth. But Alan's strongest compassion was reserved for himself.

The sun was still hanging low over the eastern horizon when Alan stepped out of his tent, but already mists were steaming out of the jungle that crowded around most of Great Chesapeake Bay. Here, though, below the highlands, was a long stretch of shining sand beach, and already lithe youngsters were scampering up the slanted trunks of the coconut palms, trying to get in the day's needs before the morning heat made strenuous work impossible. Others were out wading into the surf with nets and fishing lines. Their cheerful singsongs rang out sharp and clear as the two groups called insulting challenges to each other.

Alan paused a moment and rubbed his right shoulder, then worried at a bite just below the belt line on the curve of his right hip. He hated roughing it, but sleeping in only his own thin insulated coverpac was preferable to accepting the hospitality of a tribesman's infested pallet. Not that he had managed to escape the biters even now.

Despite his pale hair and light eyes, he was already tanned as dark as many of the tribesfolk, after a year of Buffalo's subtropical climate. He sauntered slowly down to the kitchen ring, where the women of the tribe were gathered around the remains of last night's feast—held in honor of a young hunter's first major triumph, not for the visitor from the Canadian northwest. They were breakfasting on greasy chunks of cold pork and rat. Stomach still queasy from last night's sour beer, Alan declined an invitation to join them, settling instead for a single banana and the milk from a fresh-cut coconut.

The Kelly's tent was staked out on the highest point of land in the vicinity, the rest of the encampment scattered in an unplanned halfmoon about the bottom of that short hill. The ground was clear of other tents all around the slope, and a ring of guards was posted immediately around the tent and another halfway down the slope. As chief the Kelly owned the largest tent of all, of course, perhaps eighteen feet in diameter, and the only one to be colored. They must have had tradestuff to dye the roof, for the black was intense, even sinister, as intended; but the green of the walls was mottled and in places showed where rain had made it run and rust, spoiling the attempt at elegance. The roof was topped by a spear bearing the Kelly's personal totem, the pelt of a white weasel. As always, Alan's eyes were dragged to the totem, and he inwardly shuddered. It was too easy to imagine another totem joining it—his head.

He was early, a wise precaution in all business, but most of the tribal elders were already gathered in the meeting circle, passing around gourds of beer. And being early meant that he could not refuse the vessel suddenly thrust in his face. He took as small a mouthful of the beer as possible, forcing himself not to grimace as he swallowed, and nodded in vigorous appreciation as he passed the vessel to the man on his right.

That worthy grinned and rubbed a broken tooth that protruded over a scar-tissue-thickened lower lip, and drained the gourd, belching as he finished to show his satisfaction. It was a courtesy Alan had not yet mastered. He tossed the gourd over his shoulder in the general direction of one of the women serving the council and a moment later it was returned, refilled.

"Hey, city-man!"

The man started to reach over to Alan, then paused to belch again, an even louder eruption that obviously pleased him mightily. He beamed with pleasure, but whatever he was going to say was stilled by the sudden appearance of his leader.

The Kelly stood just outside his tend for a moment, blinking at the daylight and scratching vigorously at the thatch of red hair that pushed over the waistband of his trade denim shorts. He was a giant among his own people, even though Alan had nearly three inches on him. But Alan was slender, while the chieftan bulked thick nearly everyplace. His shoulders were broad and his upper arms could have strained the belt that circled Alan's waist. The faded blue shorts and rope sandals were the only articles of clothing worn by the men, while the women wore skirts that varied from crotch to knee-length—more a support for the many pockets that they sported than a means toward modesty. Many of the skirts had originally been colorful, although they were faded now, but just as many were cut from the same trade denim.

One woman's pockets were deep enough to hold a chicken, for Alan spotted one struggling for freedom. After a moment the woman reached down and wrung its neck, her bare breasts bobbing with the twisting movement.

The Kelly yawned suddenly, empty socket closing in an obscene wink. Then he came over to plop his bulk down in his chair. The frame was made from ivory tusks, covered with a shaggy hide that Alan thought was Plains buffalo. Probably the tribe didn't know, for the thing had been looted from some long-forgotten museum. The chair served the useful purpose of keeping the chieftan mounted above his people.

The elders had fallen silent at the appearance of their leader, and remained that way until a gourd had been given to him. He used it only to rinse out his mouth, spitting out the beer in a spray that showered those to his right. He made a sound then, and wiped his mouth with the back of his hand. Then he looked straight at Alan.

"You. City-man."

Alan froze for a moment, pinned by the baleful glare from the chief's eye, made angrier by the empty socket. Then he was on his feet and bowing from the waist.

"Mighty Kelly, I bring you greetings."

"Yah." He hawked, and spat phlegm. "You come far, city-man, with no guard. You crazy, or a fool?"

Alan flushed, fingers whitening as they gripped tighter around the box. "The men from Yellowknife are not cowards, afraid to leave their mothers' skirts without the protection of an army."

The Kelly laughed. "Brave man. You die as brave when I tie you down to a stake an' shove a spear down you throat an' out you ass?"

"I didn't come here to die." Sweat was pouring down his back as he tried to will his knees to stop their quaking.

"Yah?" He looked at the seer. "Ya ken why he come, old man?"

Alan had not noticed the seer before, for the old man kept to the background, hanging behind his master. But now he came forward, pulling himself up from his squat with an obvious effort, to look the stranger in the face. Then he reached out a bony claw and lifted Alan's chin, turning his head first one way then the other. Alan forced himself not to flinch away from the garlic-laden breath.

"There's no harm here, Captain," the old man said then. "He means ye no ill."

"Yah?" The Kelly leaned forward. "You got a gift—gimme."

He had to pick his way through the council of elders—many of whom appeared to be quite young to have earned their place of respect—to hand over the box, after first loosening the lid. The barbarian stared at the pair of pistols, obviously pleased. Then he drew out the silver one, balanced it in his hand in a way that showed familiarity with the weapon, and picked out the clip. He slammed it home, then sighted down the barrel at Alan. Then without warning he pulled the trigger, and the slug slammed by Alan's head, inches from his ear.

His first instinct was to stumble back, hand clasped to the side of his head, expecting to find blood; and he did nearly fall over one of the natives. Then he realized that the Kelly was roaring with laughter, fist doubled and beating against the arm of his chair while his good eye wept under the closed lid. It took the tribesmen only seconds to pick up on the joke, each trying to outdo his master in mirth. Even Alan managed a weak grin when the Kelly at last wiped his eye and calmed a bit, although a murderous anger was churning within his guts.

"Nice toy, city-man," the barbarian said at last. "You got more bullets?"

"Not with me," said Alan. "But I can arrange for you to receive more ammunition, the next time you visit Buffalo."

"Yeah?" Suddenly there was no more mirth, even the chuckling of the elders stopping as though it had been cut off with a knifeblade. "Nobody ever give us bullets, city-man. Why you do it now?"

"You have something I want," said Alan.

"You want it awful bad—maybe I keep it, if it's that good."

"It isn't that good to you—not as good as bullets, and perhaps more guns. Think what you could do with six rifles—not old stuff, rusting and rotting so that it's more dangerous to pull the trigger than to be in front of the barrel. New guns, from Yellowknife."

The barbarian couldn't help but be interested. He rubbed his nose. "Go on, city-man. Talk more."

"You have a boy—a city-boy."

The barbarian stared blankly, and so Alan went on. "The boy was seen with you three days out of Buffalo."

The Kelly shook his head. "No boy."

"He was seen," Alan insisted. "Less than two months—two moons ago."

"No." He stood up so suddenly that his chair went over backward. "No boy. Go way, city-man. Go back to Buffalo. I got nothing you want."

He was still holding the pistol, and the box. Now he cast them down and turned to stride back to his tent, leaving the elders as surprised as Alan. He had scarcely disappeared before they were whispering among themselves, and casting furtive glances toward Alan.

As for Alan himself, the shock lasted only a few seconds. He had expected almost any sort of reaction from the barbarian—except this. He stood there a moment, staring at the Kelly's closed tent, and then wheeled and left the meeting circle. He could feel their eyes on his back until he was down the slope, and moving among the random scattering of the tents; but even when they were out of sight the knowledge that they were thinking about him was almost strong enough to color the air.

Then he was at his own tent, a native structure that had been given to him when he made it plain that he had not arrived empty-handed. It had taken hours for a bug bomb to fumigate the place before he dared move in, but it would take him only minutes to move out when the moment came.

Had that moment arrived?

There were some who would take the Kelly's dismissal at face value, but Alan was discovering an unexpected tendency toward foolhardiness in himself. Damn it, he didn't like being treated this way by an unwashed savage! He would choose his own time and manner of leaving . . .

If he could leave of his own power.

For now, though, he would double his personal armament. He was already well supplied with devices not readily apparent to the casual encounter, but he could add a safety measure. He ducked into the tent and drew out his kit; the telltales showed that there had been no further attempts at the case since his first day, when one of the tribesmen had picked up a nasty burn for tinkering with the wrong thing. The message must have gotten through clear and strong.

To join the needle-gun already strapped to his left wrist Alan chose a clip of fragmentation grenades and their launcher for his other arm. The needle-gun, and the sleepy pills behind his belt, were intended only to put the enemy out of commission without causing permanent danger. The grenades would kill if planted in the right spot. He added a knife to his boot and slipped three extra clips of grenades into the body holster that he strapped to his side, beneath his shirt, feeling a bit foolish even as he did so. He had not actually fired a weapon since leaving school, and he wondered now if even ten years of childhood training in weapons and survival conflict would prove to be enough against the practiced savagery of the tribesmen.

He paused to look up at the tent's other occupant, the hawk; wings folded back to where the tips were almost touching and talons extended to rake with hatred, it was hard to acknowledge that the bird was not still alive. But there were no hawks left alive; the species was one completely eliminated in the aftermath of world holocaust.

Alan had found this ancient specimen in an old house not twenty miles north of here—the farmer who lived there insisted that it was on the site of historical Trenton itself, although there was little evidence other than massive mounds already recaptured by the jungle that there had ever been any evidence of man's presence on the spot.

The farmer's house certainly was not that old, although it was furnished with the gleanings of two centuries of graverobbing. Of all that was in the rude house, only the stuffed hawk, mounted under a glass bell kept precariously whole for God-knew-how-many centuries, was of true value. And it was the obvious prized possession of the family.

"It was mounted by my granther's granther, and maybe his granther's granther afore him," said the farmer, and that made a probable eight generations of history—two centuries. There were those who said that that was the time of the holocaust. "Take it, city-man."

"I cannot," Alan protested. But he had saved the man's wife from the ravages of fever, thanks to his personal kit, even though the witch woman and the medicine worker alike had given her up for dead. The farmer was old, nearly forty, and could not afford a new wife. To have this one saved meant that he could live out his own days in relative peace.

And so the hawk was his, although he could not take the glass bell on horseback. Now he stared at the hate-filled eyes, wondering what the bird had been attacking—was it the man who finally brought it down to death?

He had brought the bird veiled into the barbarian camp, knowing that they would consider it a great totem. Perhaps he should have kept it that way, but he had uncovered it once, to study the look in its eyes, and then had been unable to pull the cloth over that head again. It had been troublesome wiring it up in its present position, but it did have the appearance of life.

He restored the kit to its place beneath the coverpac, but not before tripping a signal that would warn him of attempts at meddling; then he stood, ready to leave the cramped confines of the tent—scarcely wide enough to hold the coverpac in its stretched-out position. But before he could turn there was a scrabbling at the entrance, and the Kelly's far-seer was darting beetlelike through the flap.

"City-man?" Then he saw the hawk, poised to drop with its deadly claws, and a single strangled sound escaped his throat. He dove for the entrance, but Alan's outstretched foot caught him behind the knee and brought him down.

"Easy, old man." The skin-covered bones were quivering with fear. "It's not alive."

"What . . . What in the name of heaven's hell is it?"

"A bird that used to be," said Alan. "It's been a long time dead, old man. It can't hurt you."

But the old man was not at all ready to accept his assurances. He edged closer to the entrance, ready to flee if the horrible thing should show any evidence of being released from the spell that bound it.

"What is it, old one?"

"The boy, city-man. The boy y'seek. He is here—he was here."

"I know that. Where is he now?"

"Safe away, hidden. Well away, where y'canna find him w'out the the help o' the Kelly himself."

"Why?" demanded Alan. "Why does your master keep the boy hidden? I gave him a great bribe, offered more than three boys are worth. Six rifles, old man—that is a great thing for one tribe to have."

"Ay," agreed the seer. "A fortune to us—the way to a fortune. An' there are those who would gladly gi' up the one for the many, city-man. Those o' us who think straight on th' matter."

"Well, then?"

"We canna go against our master, y' said it y'self. He owns us. He's a great man, the Kelly—one of the fiercest and bravest. They'll sing lays about him."

The old man sighed, and eased himself down to a squat. "Our master is a great man, yes, w' but one failin': he has no heir. He's tried, a dozen times over with as many wives, but man among men though he be in the battle, he is not man enough to father a single child."

"He wants to make the stolen boy his heir?"

"The boy is strong, w' strong blood and strong teeth. An' he has the fire hair, same as th' Kelly h'self."

"What is the boy's name?"

"We call him Three Names—John Thomas Roger, he calls himself, each the name o' a proper man. What his name will be when he's brought into the tribe the Kelly has not told us."

Roger—Rogers. Not a name of importance in Yellow-knife, but the Rogers of Red River in the Manitoba district were clan leaders, and powerful in politics as well. It could not hurt to have their friendship, if it turned out the boy belonged to them.

"The adoption—when will it take place?"

"It would ha' been wi' the full moon, three days ago, but we heard that you were seeking the lad."

There was time then. Once the ceremony of adoption was over, the tribesmen would be blood bound to fight to keep the boy. But the nomads hated the city men, and it was highly doubtful that they would struggle hard to recover him if Alan could be away with him now—witness the fact that the old man was here now.

"Do you know where the boy is now?"

The old man shook his head. "Only the Kelly knows."

There was a radio in the kit. He could radio Buffalo, and they would relay the news to Red River, and then to the other cities, and in time the boy's relatives would hear of his safety and mount an expedition . . .

In time. But there was no time. It would be weeks before help could come from any point farther than Buffalo, even if the boy's family were rich and powerful enough to command space on an air transport.

"Old man, you are a seer. What am I going to do?"

"There is a way, city-man," he said, slowly. "Y'could best him in single combat."

"A stripped duel?"

"Ay, just you an' him, naked t' the world wi' naught but a blade to loose his life's blood."

"No way," said Alan, impatiently. Armed as he now was he would take his chances against even the Kelly, if events forced such a drastic turn of situation. But he knew that he wouldn't last a minute in a stripped duel. The Kelly would be able to crush him in his arms, a picture Alan refused to contemplate not because it would be an ignoble way to death, but because it would be so certain.

"No, there must be another way, a better way." One that would let him keep an intact hide.

"Well, perhaps there is one other course that would be successful," said the old man, slyly. Alan turned, to see him looking up at the hawk.

"Out with it, old man."

"Y'must be a might magician, city-man, to bring back a creature dead si' the holocaust. Work y' magic on the Kelly —make him a whole man, an' he'll gi' ye the boy. Ay, and anything more ye might wit."

Alan was mystified. "Explain yourself, old man. Make him whole in what way? I don't have the power to make him a father."

"No, not his seed, city-man—gi' him his eye!"

John Thomas Rogers was eighteen, and tall enough to wear a set of Alan's clothes, his own having deteriorated completely during his months of capture. And now that they were a safe hundred miles away from Chesapeake, he felt able to joke about his experiences.

"It might not have been so bad, being adopted. One of the rewards of manhood is your pick of the virgins—and as the Kelly's son, I could have as many of them as I wanted."

"You wouldn't have enjoyed them," said Alan, dryly. "One of the tests of manhood is a ritual circumcision."

"Oh." His voice fell. "They wouldn't tell me what the tests entailed. I guess I'll be content with what I've got."

"Cheer up. Remember, among the barbarians even the virgins have lice."

Dusk was falling; it was time to stop and make camp for the night, before they were caught again by the tropic suddenness of the sun's disappearance. They were following a river that led up into the mountains, a shortcut to the great western valley that led down to the Sea, the secret revealed by a grateful Kelly. And this was as good a spot as any, in a small cleft alongside the ancient preholocaust road. A brook came down from the cleft to cut its way through the ancient concrete.

It was the work of minutes to spread coverpacs on a grassy knoll, and then the boy set about preparing their supper while Alan grained down the horses, settling them for the night. Their baggage was meager, little but their kits—with what was left of the boy's—but the hawk rode in a bamboo cage behind Alan's saddle. He set the cage down carefully as he removed the saddle and brushed the horse for a moment; then he brought the cage over to the boy's fire.

"I wish you would let me have it, Alan. My father will pay you well."

Alan smiled. "He couldn't pay me enough, John."

He opened the cage and slipped the veil from the bird's head. The pose was as defiant as ever, left eye glaring red hatred at the world and its burden of men. But the other was blind, a white blankness that could not even offer the pretense of sight.

The barbarian chieftan had grunted when Alan explained that even the magical science of the city-men did not have the power to restore sight when there was no eye at all.

"You have two eyes," said the Kelly. "Gimme one."

"It would do you no good," said Alan. "It would not let you see, and it would soon wither way. I cannot give you the gift of sight, mighty Kelly—but I can give you another eye!"

It was then that he offered the eye of the hawk. The two-century-old artifice fitted the empty socket well, for scar tissue served to hold it secure. Alan could not have said that the addition made the Kelly any the less ugly, but it did change the barbarian, made him seem more complete. And the Kelly roared with delight when he saw the new image in Mara's looking glass. The fiery orb seemed to glow with life, matching the blaze of his hair. And though the two eyes were not matched, they seemed to complement each other to where it was difficult to say that either one might not be real.

The bird had been robbed twice now—first of life, and now of his unseeing sight. But Alan promised himself that he would make it up to the creature. Once back in Buffalo he would dispatch the hawk home to Yellowknife—by heaven, by air, even if it broke his purse. There, given a new hermetic casing, the hawk might last for centuries more. The blind pebble would be replaced too, with the largest and brightest fire stone that he could find, whether ruby or garnet and no matter what the cost.

Buffalo was no more than eight days away now. If he could get back in that span there might still be time to catch a boat that would take him across the sea and to Yellowknife in time for the summer holiday after all.

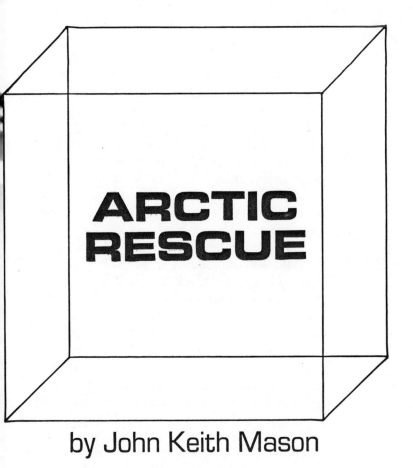

ARCTIC RESCUE

by John Keith Mason

E HAD BEEN CRAWLING through a sea of pain for hours. When the aircraft crashed, he'd been thrown clear, breaking his left leg on impact with the ice. *That* he remembered. But he must have injured his head: all memory of things before the crash was a blank.

He was in a bitterly cold place of distorted ice and snow. Making himself concentrate, he guessed the temperature must be at least 40 degrees below zero. His hands were like blocks of ice. Badly frostbitten. His face also felt frostbitten—he hardly noticed the razor-sharp wind, anymore.

With dreamlike detachment, he realized his survival was hanging by a thread.

Periodically he blacked out. Then, ensconced in a cocoon of indifference, he'd become aware of his environment—of a dull, throbbing pain-background and of a cold that was almost a burning as he crawled forward on hands and knees.

He inched his way up a slope toward a buckled pressure ridge. When he reached the top, he was gasping for breath. He paused for a moment, peering ahead. Dull, gray clouds hid the sun; his eyes kept blurring with snow blindness. Something within was impelling him in this direction —why, he didn't know. But he *did* know he would die if he stayed where he was.

Ahead, he sensed some kind of change. The wind was no longer blowing flaky snow crystals into his face. He slitted his eyes to try and see better. But all he could make out was the endless snow and ice.

He experienced a sudden surge of excitement, started crawling with renewed vigor. As he got closer to the area where he sensed a change, the conviction grew in him that this place was better for his survival, somehow.

But the effort of exerting his last strength had finished him: he collapsed in shallow snow, losing consciousness.

Kenuriak had been fishing through the ice. He'd chosen an area quite far out today and the fishing had been better than he expected. He was heading back toward land when he came upon the sprawled figure.

Alarm shot through him at sight of the other's light jacket and trousers, the obviously unlined boots. He ran forward, turned the man over. From the size of the prone form, he knew the unconscious man wasn't an Innuit. Therefore, he must be a white man.

But he wasn't. This person's skin was almost the color of fire. And the face was somehow different. At first, Kenuriak couldn't decide what was so strange. Then he noticed the nose—flat and wider than that of any white he had ever seen. Even in the books and magazines at the mission school. As he stared, he saw the nostrils were not in their normal position. They were more than three inches above the lips, almost concealed by flaps of golden skin.

Kenuriak started: the mouth was half as wide again as any in his experience.

The Innuit felt a stab of pure terror. Although it had two arms and two legs, *this thing was not a human being.*

Was it a legendary snow-demon?

Turning his attention to the ears, he shuddered. They were too high on the oddly shaped head. And of an unfamiliar tapering form. Next, he studied the fingers. Long, too thin and—he recoiled! Each hand had five fingers and *two* thumbs, one at each end. From their appearance, he guessed that the hands were frostbitten. Probably the face, too, though he didn't know what the creature's skin normally looked like.

His initial revulsion vanished. Whatever he was, this being desperately needed help.

The little man leaned forward. Working his hands beneath the body, he lifted, expecting it to be heavy. He nearly lost his grip with surprise. The other was barely half as heavy as he'd thought!

Kenuriak grinned. That simplified matters. But how could such a large individual be so light? He shook his head in perplexity.

Lifting the strange being over his shoulder, he started back across the pack ice.

Fifteen minutes later, Kenuriak reached his dog team. The huskies began snarling and straining at the leads. The Innuit shouted to his dogs, but they seemed to have gone crazy. He had to circle them warily, well out of range, to reach the sled safely.

As he wrapped the stranger in sealskins, the dark-skinned little man became thoughtful. The dogs had recognized that something was wrong with this creature. He nodded to himself: huskies always knew!

Impatiently, Kenuriak brushed the thought aside. Whatever else he might be, the other remained a fellow creature, and he was dying. The Innuit knew that as surely as he knew his own name.

Unstrapping his whip from the sled's side, he lashed the huskies into motion. There was no time to waste; his igloo was nine miles distant.

In his winter home, Kenuriak's wife, Ruthee, was afraid. She whispered, "My husband, is he a snow-demon?"

The hunter was honest. "I do not know, Ruthee. But, he *is* in urgent need of food, warmth, and medicine."

Looking carefully at the figure on the bedroll, he said, "I do not feel he is a snow-demon. Such things are never affected by cold. It is their natural element."

Reassured by her husband's conviction, the woman began running her hands over the golden-skinned body. When her fingers touched the lower left leg, she drew in her breath sharply.

"Ai! His leg is broken, my husband. In two places."

Kenuriak crouched beside her, feeling the leg. He beamed across at her.

"That *proves* it! He cannot be a snow-demon, Ruthee: they *never* suffer from broken bones. Quickly—get some hot broth into him!"

The Innuit woman was spooning steaming soup into the injured person, when his eyes opened. She almost dropped her spoon with shock. The stranger's eyes had all the changing colors of the Northern Lights!

The being from the ice pack looked with astonishment at the two small, fur-clad figures. Then he realized one of them was giving him nourishment, smiled his thanks. As consciousness faded, he felt the pain of returning circulation in hands and feet.

For three days, the golden-skinned one's life hung by a

thread. On the fourth, he awoke, feeling better. He was still weak, but he seemed to have weathered the crisis; he knew he was on the mend.

His face, hands, and feet still hurt, but now it was a healing sort of pain. When he glanced at his hands, they were covered with small skins under which he felt some kind of medicinal balm. His face and feet had also been smeared with it. And his broken leg was tightly lashed with bone splints.

He peered up to see the little dark-skinned man smiling at him. He grinned back, aware that the other was much different physically from himself. He was considerably shorter and his face wasn't quite right. The nose seemed larger than normal, the hair—what he could see of it in the sputtering light of the oil lamp—unusual in texture. Still, the sick man knew that this odd little fellow and his wife had saved his life.

Kenuriak squatted beside the other. The Innuit said, "Strange One, I know not how we shall talk, but you are welcome in my igloo. When I found you on the ice, you were nearly dead. My wife, Ruthee, has nursed you, day and night, for four days."

The peculiar eyes looked surprised. The sick one drew himself upon one elbow with excitement. *He had understood the little man.* The words were completely alien, but their meaning became clear a split-second after the other spoke. At that moment, the veil drew back from his memory. *He knew who he was and where he had come from.*

The stranger's eyes fixed upon Kenuriak. His lips didn't move, but deep in the Innuit's mind a voice said:

Don't be afraid, my brother. I speak to you, mind-to-mind. When you answer, just look into my eyes and speak slowly and clearly.

Kenuriak stared with utter amazement at the other.

He said, "How is it that I understand you? You are a person from so far away that I have never seen your like, even in the books and magazines of the mission school."

The stranger's face lit up with a radiant smile.

Kenuriak the Innuit, you don't realize how right you are. I come from a place not of this world—a place beyond the stars.

The little man darted an astonished look at his wife.

"He speaks to me from inside my own head!" he cried.

Ruthee was terrified.

"My husband," she shrieked, "he *is* a snow-demon!"

She turned a horror-filled look upon the golden-skinned being. But a soothing sensation spread throughout her body-mind, causing her fear to ebb. Like the tinkling of sleigh bells, a voice in her mind said:

Ruthee, my sister, I would no more hurt you, or Kenuriak, than I would harm my own father or mother. You saved my life; we are linked as mind-companions, and shall be as long as we both shall live.

The woman gaped at her husband.

"His words are inside my head, too!"

Kenuriak soothed her, "I know, Ruthee. I heard, this time. It is strange, but he means us well. Do not fear."

Turning to the other, "What is your name, Strange One?" he inquired politely.

Teealis, my brother.

"How is it that you were so easy to carry back on the ice?"

The world I come from has matter which is not so dense as on your world, Kenuriak. Thus my weight is much less than a man of the same size from your planet.

"How did you come to be alone and dying on the ice pack?"

The power failed in my flyer. When it crashed, I was

*thrown clear, breaking my leg on the ice. My machine
sank into the ocean beneath. But my head was also injured,
causing me to forget who I was and where I came from.*

Kenuriak looked bewildered.

"These things are hard for me to understand. Did you
come from this far place in your flyer, without any companions?"

Teealis laughed.

*No, I came with other comrades in a great starship. I
wanted to study the pack ice from a low level, so I took a
small flyer such as we use on planets like this. But I made
a serious mistake: I forgot to refuel before leaving the
mothership.*

The Innuit looked reprovingly at Teealis.

"That is the sort of silly thing a green boy does!"

The golden-skinned being looked sheepish.

*Kenuriak, I am a green boy. I'm only fifteen. This is my
first trip to another planet in a distant star system.*

The Innuit looked flabbergasted.

"I am sorry. I did not realize . . ."

The other smiled.

*. . . that I was so young because my race is bigger than
the Innuits? Don't apologize. It was a foolhardy thing
to do.*

The dark-skinned hunter looked worried.

"But how can we let your companions know that you are
alive and safe?"

Teealis indicated the belt at his waist.

I have the means for that.

He pressed a stud on the belt. A loud humming filled
the igloo, then faded away.

Kenuriak looked wide-eyed at him.

"Is this like the white man's radio which sends messages
to far places?"

Teealis nodded.

It will guide my people here. Are the white men even in the Arctic?

The little man looked sad.

"Oh, yes. With their airplanes and other wonderful machines, they control everything."

Teealis peered anxiously at the Innuit.

You haven't informed them about finding me, have you?

The dark-skinned hunter laughed.

"Informed them? How could I? I have no radio."

The other looked relieved.

I'm certainly glad of that. I would've been in real trouble if the whites knew of my presence. As it is, I'll still have some explaining to do about losing the flyer.

An hour later, a disk-shaped flyer landed in front of the igloo. Three huge golden-skinned beings stepped from a hatch that opened in its side. Their leader broke into a run at sight of Teealis, waving to him from Kenuriak's sled.

There were tears in his eyes as he embraced the youth. Then for long moments they looked at each other in the way of their race while Teealis told his father all that had happened since the crash. Finally, the spaceman rose to his enormous height, and advanced to meet Kenuriak, hand extended.

At the same time, one of the other big men moved over to examine Teealis. He studied, with interest, the healing balm on his face and hands, nodded approvingly, as if to say—he's all right!

Taking the strange, long fingers in his, Kenuriak smiled up at the spacemen. As the other's eyes locked with his, the Innuit heard a deep voice in his mind:

My son has told me how you saved his life, Kenuriak. I am Corteel. I thank both you and your wife for your great kindness to one of an alien race, one so different from your-selves. We had thought him dead since losing contact with the flyer.

The Innuit looked embarrassed. Praise always made him uncomfortable. Perceiving this, the other changed the subject.

Teealis tells me you are of the Innuit people.

The small man nodded gravely.

"It is our name for our people. The white men call us Eskimos, but that is an Indian word, and not correct. What are your people called, Corteel?"

The big man smiled.

We are the Varonians of Kalgor, a world far out in the stars.

Kenuriak looked awed.

"These things are very strange to me. Have you come to take over from the whites?"

The Varonian looked amused.

No, Kenuriak. We're only here to study those who control this world. You see, the whites will soon be developing star travel themselves; my people want to know what kind of problems they will bring with them when they journey to the stars.

The Innuit gazed long at the other.

"Have your people solved the problem of war, Corteel?" he asked.

The spaceman nodded solemnly.

We have. And those who control this planet will also have to resolve that problem before they will be allowed to join our interstellar union of races.

The small hunter grinned widely.

"Our white brothers will have some *very* interesting days ahead of them."

The spaceman nodded. Then, turning to his companions, he gestured toward the flyer. The other two picked Teealis up, started carrying him toward the open hatch. But the youth stopped them, beckoned the Innuit. Kenuriak and Corteel came to him.

Looking into the dark-skinned hunter's eyes, Teealis said:

I will tell the people of my world how you saved me from death on the ice pack; how Ruthee's nursing brought me back to life. When the whites of Earth reach us in their starships, perhaps they will hear the saga of Kenuriak, the Innuit, and his Arctic rescue. Farewell, my friend!

The last thing Teealis saw from the flyer's port as it lifted from this land of distorted ice and snow was the tiny, fur-clad figure of Kenuriak, waving goodbye. He watched until it disappeared in the whiteness below.

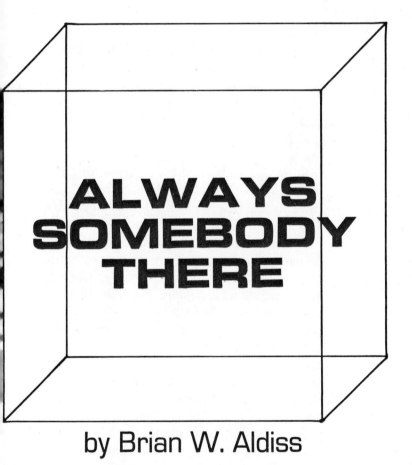

ALWAYS SOMEBODY THERE

by Brian W. Aldiss

THE STARSUB HAD TRAVELED farther than any other material thing in the history of the universe. Its quest was so abstruse that the objective could be expressed only in mathematical symbols; to put it into words, one would have to say that the starsub had been in search of the Creator.

It had not found the Creator and was returning home.

So long had it been away, traversing its own particular dark variant of space and time, that the universe had changed mightily in its absence. The starsub itself was changed.

There were two occupants of the starsub, a maner and a comput. They were not readily distinguishable, except that the maner was organic and the comput inorganic. For many epochs, the maner had been held in deep-freeze, only three degrees Kelvin above BAZ, or Biological Activity Zero. Now that the starsub was about to materialize in space/time, he roused from a long-protracted dream about a gigantic statue which stood amid eternal snow, and went to the control room to seek out the comput.

The comput was more shadowy than the maner, the planes of its face slatey and hard to focus upon, for its most vital workings stretched into several dimensions inaccessible to human vision. It turned slowly and stared at the maner.

"So, Gor, you return to the level of consciousness. By the reckoning of these instruments, you have been away in near-BAZ for some five million, nine hundred and eighty-three thousand-odd decades. Allowing for relativistic distortions of time, that must represent the life and death of the entire universe outside."

"The life, death, and possible rebirth of the universe," said Gor. He spoke slowly, so slowly that the comput asked, "And you, are you alive or dead?"

"Neither at present, An. My head is still surfeited with a long dream, which filled my brain for all those countless millions of decades of nonexistence. I saw—I was—someing like a gigantic statue, standing amid eternal snows. So mighty was I that I could banish the snow for a while, yet always more fell. Though I was made of a substance more enduring and immutable than granite, yet I had some limited movement. I felt in consequence as if I were at once omnipotent and yet powerless. And I was all alone."

The comput looked ahead through the blank port and said, as if to itself, "That is a dream of one beyond the reach of life and death, and typical of deep-freeze, I would judge. Better that than to be as me, awake and aware for all those millions of empty decades."

Gor moved slowly over to the control console. Turning his head, he said, "Do you suffer, An?"

"That is a human term. I have gone insane. I shall not function when we end our journey; my coherent being will terminate."

"Do not speak so. Though we failed to discover the Creator, yet you and I have more knowledge than any other entities in the entire universe. You are therefore invaluable."

"Nothing is invaluable that is not valued. We know nothing of the universe we have entered. All our painfully acquired knowledge may amount to ignorance if basic laws have changed."

By now, the projectile that encased them had so transmuted and damped down its energies that it slid from the abstract continuum in which it had journeyed, emerging into the ordinary space/time of the universe.

With a feat of memory that came to him as if buried beneath deep strata of rock, Gor the maner pressed the correct wells on the console before him. Great metal eyelids that covered the forepart of the starsub slid away, and the world of space and suns and planets was revealed to them.

Both organic and inorganic creatures stood staring through the ports for a long while without speech.

An the comput said, "It was no idle word I spoke when I mentioned my insanity. Time deforms all things. What I see beyond our vessel is not space but flaring reds and greens."

"I too am insane," said Gor.

For him also, space was a crazed affair of flags, of great rippling banners in gaudy primary colors which filled the entire firmament. There was nothing that could be called darkness, nothing that could be called space, only great flaring strips of color with eternities for flagpoles.

"The basic laws have changed," An said.

The colors were unbearable. He closed the shutters again, turning with infinite sloth to the instrumentation.

The instrumentation indicated that solid bodies still existed, even in this impossible universe. Between them, the two beings set a course for the nearest body which had a mass approximately that of the Earth—the planet they had left such an incomputable while ago.

With only a slight jolt, the starsub settled on the unknown world. As it became stationary, so did An. The mysterious planes of it dissolved; it remained where it was, lifeless, faceless.

Gor was beyond emotion. He reopened the metal eyelids and began to observe the world on which he had landed. As far as he could judge, it was little bigger than the games field on which he had played—the phrase if not the memory returned to him—when he was a boy.

Taking his time, he climbed into a metal suit, the life-support systems of which would guarantee his survival, he hoped, for a while at least. Leaving An mute at the controls, he walked through the ship's only exit and stood on the surface of the unknown world.

It appeared to him that the world was octahedral, but this was possibly a distortion of his sense of sight—the starsub was an unrecognizable object. He looked at the vessel in fascination and observed that it was dwindling. With patient observation, it could be seen to shrink. Gor watched, trying to understand what was happening. Eventually, he decided that, in this universe, time was as much a regular dimension as height or length; in consequence, a passage of time suffered from dwindling perspective just as much as a passage in space. Already, the starsub was too small for him to reenter.

With his senses still dulled and slowed by near-BAZ, he had stood motionless on the world for longer than he could reckon. The bright flapping colors were fading from the sky, the great flags becoming filmy.

About him, nothing stood, nothing moved. He could use none of his vast store of knowledge; there was nothing to use it on.

As the gaudy hues of the universe faded, Gor could perceive other worlds in what—for want of a better term—he thought of as space. They were all octahedral, and shone with the sullen glow of pewter. Some were pockmarked.

And some bore life.

It was life of a kind. Gor cast about in his great slow mind for a word, trundling it at last out of a dark corner: kangaroo. Somewhere back in another universe had been a creature called a kangaroo. There were now creatures like kangaroos. That is to say, there were creatures with long angled legs which hopped, or so it appeared. But they were two-headed, and their heads grew on the ends of their legs. They possessed no tails. They were blue and feathered. They hopped from one world to another.

There was no joy in their progress, as one creature followed another, for now the colors had faded into no more than a ghostly background to space, and a stream of white ash fell everywhere.

As they moved from globe to globe, hopping, hopping, never stopping, the creatures gave out a thin piping noise.

Extending all his senses beyond fatigue, beyond knowledge, beyond his age-old dream, Gor listened to their cry, and discerned what it was they cried.

"We're a-cold! We're a-cold! Where has all the warmth, sweet warmth, gone?"

And then he understood something of the real extent of the time that he had been lost and gone. Not only had his old familiar universe suffered death and dissolution; he had slept all through the lifespan, the incalculable eons, of the succeeding universe. He had arrived back in time to witness its last pallid flickerings before it too went the way of even the most enduring of things.

The kangaroo creatures became fewer, fainter. The ash that fell like snow came down more thickly, the light became more sickly.

He stood there, neither alive nor dead. His head was still full of the long dream which had nourished his brain for countless millions of decades. As the octahedron shrank beneath him, he stood more and more like a gigantic statue amid eternal snows.

So mighty did he become as the universe itself dwindled, that he could banish the snows for a while. Yet always more fell.

Now he knew himself to be of a substance more enduring than any material substance. Yet he was scarcely able to move: the death of time and space had brought stasis. In consequence, he felt himself to be at once omnipotent and powerless. He was entirely alone.

Slowly, slowly, infinitely slowly, he bent down and scooped up a handful of the snowy ash. Everything else continued to diminish.

Unaware of whether he woke or dreamed, he began clumsily to fashion a new universe.

DEATH OR CONSE-QUENCES

by Sonya Dorman

ELLO, SANDRA, HELLO SANDRA," the man keeps saying to me and I open my eyes. I'm too hot.
My mother's gone somewhere. Where? "Hello,
Sandra." He has such a low voice, G, perhaps:
a voice like a cello.

"Hello," I say. I'm hot and aching. But I know
who I am. Sandra Holland, seventeen, blue eyes,
mouse-brown hair, next month my first concert
at the Dallas Auditorium. Why am I so strange,
lying here?

"Where am I?" I ask, as the man bends over
me, gives me a shot of some kind, in the upper
arm. His voice is beautiful and mature, like
Brahms. I think I'm not thinking so well. "Am I
in Houston?"

"No," the man says. "All the Cryos were moved
to Sagittarius many years ago." He puts an im-
personal arm under my shoulders, and helps me
to sit up. I'm in a small room, in a boxlike sort
of recliner; two others, empty, stand near mine,
each one visible clearly in the glow of light from
some fixture above it.

My God, I'm a vampire, I think. My mother's
Roumanian, and vampires are a sort of joke in
the family. "Fey, fair woman," my father calls
her. I play for her when she sings, which is good
discipline, because when I play alone I can soar

off by myself, but when I must hew to her line it's much harder, and then we love each other more.

The man is writing, doing it with a piece of metal on a sheet which isn't paper.

"What's a Cryo?" I ask.

He puts down his implements and looks at me, quietly.

"May I have a cup of tea?" I ask.

"Tea?" he says, coming around to my side. "Do you think you can get up?"

He helps me lean forward in my box, (no stake in my heart, I'm not a vampire). The recliner swings down and dumps me on my feet. I'm scared, I'm lonely, I'm seventeen and allowed to have a Martini with the family and my best friend plays the violin and studies with a student of Heifitz and I own all of Wanda Landowska's harpsichord recordings. The man leads me gently by the arm into a brilliantly lighted room which hurts my eyes for a moment.

"Here," he says, and hands me a cup of something hot. It isn't tea, but it tastes all right, rich and rather thick, like a good soup. He's looking down to a kind of tabletop, where print runs through a panel of pale green light. I guess it's a record of mine, perhaps my school marks.

The room has no windows. Light comes from oblongs near the top; there are many cabinets; his flat, long desk. Not even an ashtray on it, but perhaps he doesn't smoke. His face is round and pale, not very interesting. I won't tell him how frightened I am.

"Well, then," he says, and turns off the running stream of print, and I remember that in physics I only get eighty, though my other marks were good. But I'm in love with Mr. Harwin. No, it isn't that, even I know better, it's just that I'm crazy about him. It makes it hard to concentrate on physics, to feel so physical about the instructor. I sit in the physics lab and think: Howard Harwin, I wish you would instruct me, how much I wish it. He could have given me an eighty-five, just for love.

The man is nodding in agreement with whatever he has read. "Sandra," he says, and looks up at me, but I don't like his eyes when I meet them, they say nothing. "Piano, flute, and classical guitar," he says.

"Yes," I say. "Where am I? What's a Cryo?"

"You're in the annex to the Sagittarius Rehabilitation Hospital," he answers. "In a moment I'll take you in to meet your doctor."

"Sagittarius was The Archer. Why do I need a doctor?"

"I believe he was modeled on Chiron, who was a medical advisor, among other things." His voice is perfectly neutral, like his eyes. "You have no recall?"

I say, "No, I don't. Nothing. I'm going to give my first concert next month," and my voice falters, because I know things have changed, there won't be any concert, I'm still crazy about Howard and I can purse my lips for a kiss or the flute but I know I'm not likely to get either.

The man puts his hands down flat on the desk. "That's unusual, no recall of anything," he says, and I swallow hard. As if people weren't always telling me something about me is unusual: my talent, my brains, my legs which are too fat and my love for Howard Harwin which is ninety percent sexual longing and what's worse and so unusual is I know it. "Please tell me what's happened," I say.

"In 1970 the doctors diagnosed leukemia," the man says

by rote, with his eyes half-shut, "and in the terminal stage your parents put you into Freeze against a future time when a cure and guarantee of health could be found for you, against which they left an insurance policy which was paid out to Texas Freeze, Incorporated, at the rate of three hundred and fifty dollars per month . . ." he turns on the printed record again and continues, ". . . and their love and hope that you will mature into a fine musician . . ." he's dancing in front of my blurry eyes because I know that's how my mother would have written it, and read it aloud to my father for his approval, ". . . and bring to audiences of the future . . ."

"All right!" I scream. "No more. Don't read any more." My voice goes under when I start to ask, "What . . ." and I stop, breathe, try again. "What are they playing now?"

"I beg your pardon?" he says.

My God, I think, *where* am I? "What music are they playing now?"

He sighs. He opens and shuts the top drawer of his desk. "This is simply a hospital, Miss Holland," he says. "We do not have any live entertainment here. I must get you in to see your doctor," and he stands up.

I noticed before there were no windows in this room, but now I really take note of it, and the warmth I felt after drinking the cup of hot liquid is gone, except for my eyes and throat, which are scalding.

"It was felt you were one of the special potentials," he says.

"I don't know what you mean."

"They were not able to transfer all the Cryos when storage became such a problem," the man says, his flat eyes looking hard at me. "Only those judged to be of particular value are here."

"What did they do with the others, let them melt?" I ask, my grief turning to outrage and shame.

"Now," he says, taking me gently by the arm, "now come and see your doctor. He'll be able to answer many of your questions."

He opens another door and we go into a corridor. As soon as we step on the designed portion of the floor, it begins to move, taking me by surprise, and I gasp and grab at his arm to steady myself. The hall moves us at a slow, dignified speed for a minute, and then we step off and go through another doorway into another windowless, lighted room.

Here sits a giant of a man. His hair is a thin, dark fringe around his skull, his eyes are heavy-lidded, and when they look at me they say everything, as my father's did: little girl, you're scared, you're full of questions, trust me and I'll soothe you and make you well and give you the score for a concerto no one has ever played.

We're left alone facing each other, and I say nothing, but sit in the chair he indicates for me. He presses a desk panel which lights up and my records—medical, not academic, I realize—run before him. While he reads them he sits perfectly still, with his forearms on the desk. He's wearing some simple suit or uniform of a pale, pearl gray which is pleasant to look at.

At last I ask, "What's going to happen to me?"

"You will live," he replies without looking up.

"That wasn't what I meant."

He releases the panel and it goes dark. "After about two weeks of intensive blood-chemistry alteration, and rehabilitation, you'll be placed in a town or city of your own choice, or at a university. That is, if you wish to continue certain studies, you may do so. I imagine there are other questions you'd like to ask?"

While he speaks I'm winding up tighter, my voice is getting thinner, and I'm in a kind of dry-eyed rage which masks my panic when I say, "I'm glad to hear there are still music schools, in whatever year this is."

"They may not be like the ones you knew. The year is 2108."

"Why did it take so long?"

"To find a cure for leukemia? It didn't. You're hardly the first off the line, you know." The open, friendly eyes are raised to my face. "We have actually accomplished very little, compared to the hopes of people of your time."

"I meant star travel. We're on another planet."

The doctor gives a sigh, pushes his seat back, and gets up. "You'll have a few weeks of orientation, as well as medical attention," he says. "We're not on a planet. Sagittarius is one of a dozen specialized satellites in orbit around Earth. None of the planets was sufficiently hospitable to colonize and Earth is fearfully overcrowded. We've come to look on satellites as sort of stationary spaceships."

"And then what happens?" I ask, feeling myself getting too tight. Someone with a big hand, Doctor God, is turning the peg until I twang.

"The piano, the flute, and the classical guitar," the doctor says in a mild voice. "Here we have sutures, organ banks, and biochemists." As he says "here" he describes a small circle with one hand. "Out there," he says, and he makes a big circle, "when you're ready, you'll find something for yourself. You're so much younger than most of the Cryos, it may be easier for you."

"Are you telling me there isn't any music? I don't believe it."

"Sure there is," he says, and touches something on his desk. A zippy little electronic tune fills the air, impertinent, repetitive, recognizable even here, even in this year, to my ears, as a popular song.

Other times, perhaps dreaming of Howard, perhaps riding in the car with my parents, I would enjoy it. But I make a face. The doctor turns it off. He takes my hand, guiding it to another button, presses our thumbs on it, and into the room pours a Tschaikovsky concerto played by Glenn Gould. It goes into my heart like a knife, it's the coup de grace. I faint before the tears have filled my eyes.

When I wake up, I'm in bed. In a real one, just like the ones I slept in long ago. Sitting on the edge of it is a girl perhaps two years older than I am, with bright blonde curls, and she's smiling.

"Hello, Sandra. I'm Reeny," she says.

I struggle up among the pillows. There's another bed in the room, hers, I guess, with the covers rumpled and spools of tapes piled on the table beside it, and a framed picture of a terribly handsome man. The room is small with dark walls, but it's well-lighted, comfortable, though the walls have a faint and peculiar curve at the top.

Reeny's holding something in her hand. She lifts it to her mouth, the round end sticks out in front of her face, and the mouthpiece, which doesn't seem to have a reed, is small and flat. Her lips pucker for the first note, and mine pucker in sympathy and I breathe out with her for the first sound. It's like a bead of silver, then another, four more, a whole necklace of them.

"Please give me that!" I cry, and she laughs. She wipes the mouthpiece on her robe, which is soft pearl gray, like the doctor's clothes. I lift the thing and try to blow a note, but no sound comes. Reeny watches me, and laughs again.

"Oh, here," she says, and takes the index finger of my right hand, and shows me where to press. I put the mouthpiece back in my mouth, I breathe just so, I press with my finger. The whole necklace swoops out mechanically into the air.

"It's a fake," I say, and put it down.

"No, it's a flimble," Reeny says. "It can play eight or nine pieces."

"It plays, you don't play it. I don't want something that plays by itself."

Reeny frowns. She looks at the flimble, and she looks at me. "I'm sorry, Sandra. I never met a Cryo before, so I don't know what the problems are. But we can solve them."

I lie down and look at the faint curve of the wall near the ceiling. I'm a Cryo, yes, I am. Cry-O, I say with my lips. O, cry, Sandra, maybe you're as fake as all the rest, a tune played by a pushed button.

While I lie there grieving, memories begin to seep back into my mind. Perhaps it's the familiar smell of the place, though it doesn't look anything like the hospital I remember. I was going to die.

"They'll be doctoring you soon, I think," Reeny says. "Can I do anything for you first? Can I answer any questions, maybe?"

"No, thanks," I say. I was going to die, and my parents had me frozen, and I'm still alive, in a metal ball, part of a fake Zodiac, going round and round. The family's gone, and the flute, and mice have probably eaten the felt from the piano hammers. If there are any mice left. I begin to sob.

Reeny jumps off her bed and rushes over to look down at me. "Listen," she says, sounding furious. "You know why I'm here? We smashed up our flyer," she gestures at the framed picture of the handsome man. "We were so smashed up we were like pudding. But they sorted us out, bone by bone, and put us together into our own shapes, and I can leave next week. I'm missing a few parts, because there's never enough in the banks, and so is Denn.

But life's worth it, at any price, and you make me sick. Whoever you were, you're one of the few who's getting a second chance."

Life at any price? I wonder, and try to control my crying.

"See?" Reeny says, and she lifts up the pearl gray robe, over her head. "There wasn't enough flesh anywhere," she says, her voice muffled in the gray folds. I can see that she has only one breast, and one of her shoulders is just skin and bone, with the working tendons almost showing through. She pulls the robe down around her. "At any price," Reeny says fiercely. "I'm glad to be alive. What if the flimble's a fake? There're real flutes around, if you want one. I bet you never even said thanks to the doctor."

It's true, I never did. I wasn't feeling very thankful then.

"Are you sure there are real ones?" I ask.

"Well I should hope so. They've even got real horses in the zoos."

"Have you been there?"

"There? Where? To the zoo? Sure I have. It's not bad, if you get on line early."

There's a knock at our door, and Reeny scuttles back across the room and into her bed, saying, "That's your doctor." She calls, "Come in," and then she says, "Oh, Denn, it's you." The part of his face that I can see is blank. It's plastic. Will they finish him off, or will he always be like this?

"Hi, he says to me, and the flesh part smiles, but that half of his face is only a shallow resemblance to his picture, the flesh is just a gesture. Under the plastic film of the other half there's the dark shadow of an eye socket. He touches it with his fingers. "They'll have me done in another month," he explains.

Reeny says proudly, "It took three weeks to do the first

half," and I understand they're rebuilding his face right from—what, bone? or is the skull structure platinum or plastic? or something I never ever heard of?

He bends over Reeny and kisses her, and I wonder how it feels, a half-plastic kiss. I wonder why they couldn't build her another breast, is a breast superfluous? My breasts tingle with fear.

Then my doctor comes in, not the big man I met before, but another, with the same quiet, steady eyes. "Hello, Sandra," he says. "Are you ready?"

"No," I say. "I'm scared. I'm not ready for anything, please."

"That's all right. We'll fix you up, and you'll be fine."

"She wants a real horse," Reeny says, and laughs.

Quizzically, the doctor smiles down at me. "Horse?"

"Reeny means a flute. Or piano. Or a steak, a steam engine, a bird flying," my voice beginning to run away, like a long, thin thread unwinding from me, from a spool on which all my being has been wound. Faster, faster, unwinding, until I'll be left nothing but a naked spool. "I want to see the moon shining on a lake, or my mother," he slides the needle into my arm. "Am I going to live forever?" I ask.

He bends down close so I can hear him with my fading ears. "Nobody can do that yet, but who knows?" he says. He puts a palm on my forehead, warm and dry, and it comforts me. "Go to sleep, little girl," he says. "You'll live for a long, long time."

Okay, I think, as I feel myself fading away all over. Everybody here must be missing one thing or another. I have my brain and my body.

"See you later," Reeny says, from far away.

"Play me a tune," I ask. As I begin to fall into the deeps, Reeny plays the flimble with its sad tune, little silver beads which stretch out to drops, to dashes, to long, shining lines of white silk, and just when I think I'm gone, I'm totally asleep, I hear Denn and Reeny speaking together. It's like a flash of sunlight right at the edge of the world, real human voices.

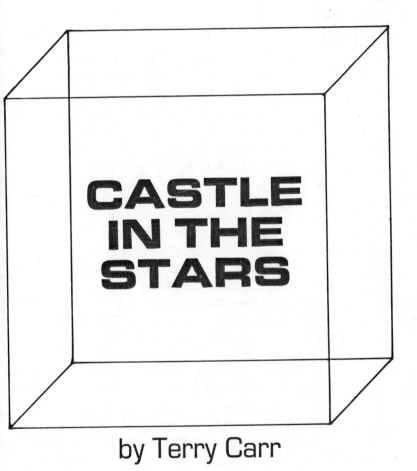

CASTLE IN THE STARS

by Terry Carr

"THIS PLANET IS UNREAL," Robeson said quietly. "Everything's too big. Those crystal forests we saw yesterday must have been a hundred feet tall, and now we find a dead beach where the sand dunes are five times that high."

"But no ocean," I said. "The planet's been dead for thousands of years. We're not going to find anything left."

Al Stoddard said, "Yes we will. I can feel it—can't you? Whatever beings were here may be long dead, but their buildings must have been *huge;* even their pocket toys would be big by our standards. They can't have been completely buried—we'll find something."

We flew over the empty beach in our tiny hover-craft, Robeson at the controls, Stoddard and I sitting behind him peering out through molecular-glass windows at the landscape below. We were in the morning zone of the planet, the dim red sun spreading faint shadows across the great empty beach below and splashing pink light on our faces. Stoddard's face seemed lit by more than that sun; excitement brightened his youthful features and his eyes glinted with anticipation.

Stoddard was the youngest of us three, a tow-haired teenage prodigy who'd graduated from the Stellar Academy with honors just weeks before. When Ozma-Nine's gravity readers had traced a series of messages to this unknown planetary system halfway around the galaxy, Stoddard had been assigned to our star probe team. Fresh out of the Academy, Stoddard expected miraculous finds to turn up immediately.

"We can't be sure there ever was any life here," Robeson said, a touch of impatience in his voice. The gray of his hair was tinted pink in the faint sun's light, the deep lines of his face black and harsh. "Most of those gravity readings turn out to be from perturbations in the star itself."

"We just check them out," I said. "Don't get your hopes up, Al." I felt kind of protective about Stoddard: he reminded me of myself twenty years ago, so eager, so expectant. A dreamer.

We all started out that way. Experience taught us better —humanity had been searching the galaxy for signs of intelligent life for nearly a century, but the most we'd ever found had been a honeycombed planet in the Kateley system whose inhabitants had burrowed deep beneath the crust when their star had died. By the time we'd found their remains, there was too little left even to establish that they'd been intelligent.

Stoddard grinned at me. "I *feel* it, that's all. There was life here once, a whole civilization. And we'll find the evidence. They were *big*, Akim."

"Everything's big here," I said. "But artifacts don't last as long as you think. What do you expect to find, some giant castle? Look, Al, we've found whole planets that were worn smooth as Olympic ice, just by the passage of time."

"High-gravity planets," he said. "The mass of this planet is so low that . . ." Suddenly his eyes widened and he pointed out the port. "Look there! Ahead of us!"

I looked, and so did Robeson. Something reared up from the dry beach—something huge and pink-tinted in the morning light. It wasn't like the sand-drifted wastes that stretched to the horizon; it reared sharply into the air and threw a long gray shadow across the dimly lit sandstone.

"I knew it!" Stoddard said. "I told you!"

Robeson grunted noncommittally. "We'll check it out," he said.

He canted the hovercraft to the right, heading for the strange upthrust. I peered ahead, fighting down a feeling of excitement that I knew had been caused by Stoddard's enthusiasm rather than by anything rational. It would be nothing, a granite column or some freak of ancient volcanic activity. But my heart was suddenly pounding.

As we approached I saw that it was unmistakably a building, some sort of structure erected by beings of intelligence. Its walls rose vertically from the beach; there was a walkway or balcony around the top, and a dark hole near the bottom that must have been an entrance gate.

Robeson was silent as he guided the hovercraft over the top of the building. Looking down, we saw rose-tinted parapets surrounding the top, drifts of sand softening the lines of the balcony. Parts of the balcony wall seemed to have eroded; they were uneven, lumpish.

The structure stood at least two hundred feet high.

Robeson curled the hovercraft around after we'd passed over the building, and we headed back toward it. He still hadn't said anything. I realized suddenly that I was holding my breath, and I let it out with a rush.

"We've got to land," Stoddard said. "We *are* going to explore it, aren't we, Captain?"

Robeson nodded. He brought the hovercraft in to a soft antigrav landing near the "front" of the building—the side where we'd seen the shadowed entrance.

"Suit up," said Robeson, and the three of us fitted our air-bubbles over our heads. In a moment I heard soft white-sound on our radio line as Robeson switched on his throat mike. "Ready?" he asked, looking over his shoulder at Stoddard and me.

"Let's go!" said the boy, reaching for the latch of the hovercraft's door. I doublechecked the reading of his air meter, then nodded to Robeson.

He pressed a button and the door irised open. We stepped out onto the hard-packed ground and stood for a moment looking up at the alien building. From here, near its base, it seemed even more mysterious than it had from the air; it was massive and foreboding, its walls unmarked by any decoration. It seemed to have been built of the same gray sandstone that surrounded it.

Stoddard started for the dark entrance eagerly, taking long, low strides in the light gravity of the planet. Robeson and I followed a bit more slowly, studying the structure as we approached it.

It was completely barren, ancient and deserted. Only the pink highlights of the morning sun high on the parapets gave it any semblance of life.

I heard someone chuckling on the radio line, and then Stoddard said, "Didn't you say something about finding a castle here, Akim? Well, here it is!"

It didn't look like a castle to me; it was huge but crudely constructed, more a giant's shack than a fortress. But it was more than we'd ever found before, anywhere in the galaxy. I followed Stoddard and Robeson to the entrance, plodding incongruously in the light gravity.

The entrance was as crude as the rest of the building. Whatever methods of construction these aliens had used, they hadn't produced very exact angles; the doorway seemed to lean to the right. The corners were rounded, and not evenly.

Well, I thought, why should an alien castle conform to our ideas of symmetry? And who could say how badly the structure had been eroded through the millennia?

Robeson paused as we came to the entrance. He put out a gloved hand to touch the rough wall. "How could a race that built so badly ever learn to control their sun's gravity?" he said.

"Maybe they built this sometime earlier," I said. "It could be centuries older than the technology they developed to send signals out to the stars."

"Maybe they *didn't* send out any signals after all," Stoddard said happily. He stood gazing up at the high building in unconcealed awe. "Maybe it was like you said, Captain— the readings we got were just random perturbations in the star. It doesn't matter, does it? They built *this*, and we've found it."

Robeson glanced wryly at me. His face was partly obscured within his air-bubble, but we'd worked together long enough for me to be able to interpret his expressions from hazy hints.

Robeson said, "Come on," and led us into the entrance.

The light of the dim sun faded quickly as we went in; we switched on our suit lights and they formed a nimbus of brightness around each of us, driving back the eons-old darkness of the corridor. The walls in here were even rougher than those on the outside, and rocky rubble was strewn over the uneven floor. There were no doorways off that corridor, only blank walls.

We walked on in silence; over my radio I heard the quiet

breathing of Stoddard and Robeson. The darkness receded before us, revealing only more rubble-strewn corridor.

Then, abruptly, the corridor ended.

There was nothing but a blank sandstone wall before us, as crude and featureless as the rest of the building. We stopped and stared in silence, then Robeson went forward and ran his gloves over the curved wall. It was all of a piece—no evidence of any kind of closed doorway.

"This doesn't make sense," Robeson said softly.

Stoddard and I went to stand beside him, and we too touched the dead-end wall in wonder. Why would anyone, human or alien, build an entrance corridor that led nowhere?

I had an idea. I turned around and began to retrace our steps toward the outside. But this time I was looking overhead, at the high ceiling of the corridor.

"You're looking for an opening up there?" Robeson said as he followed me.

"Maybe they flew," I said.

"Hey, he could be right!" said Stoddard, and the three of us walked all the way back through the corridor, gazing upward.

But the ceiling was blank, nothing but crudely shaped stone. We came to the entrance again, went outside and stood looking up at the flat facade of the giant building. Robeson switched off his suit lights with an angry motion, and Stoddard and I switched off ours too. Dim shadows sprang out along the ground.

"It's a false entrance," Robeson said at last.

I nodded. "But why?"

"How should I know?" he said. "They were *aliens*, remember? Who knows why some alien creature that lived thousands of years ago would have done anything?"

Stoddard's face seemed to swim into a smile within his

pink-tinted air-bubble. "Maybe it's a tomb," he said. "Remember the pyramids in Egypt, back on Earth? They sealed up the entrance after they buried their dead."

"No," I said. "That corridor wasn't sealed; it just *ended.*"

We stood before the huge building, listening to each other breathe. Finally Robeson said, "All right, if that wasn't the entrance then there must be one somewhere else." He started walking along the base of the building, looking all the way up and down the walls as he went. Stoddard and I followed him.

We went all the way around the building. It was pentagonal, and on the fourth of the five walls we spotted something, a dark shadow high in the wall, near the top. We stopped and stared up at it: it was a depression of some kind, but we couldn't be sure whether it was a planned feature of the building or just an irregularity in the rough surface of the wall. It must have been nearly two hundred feet above us.

"Maybe they *did* fly," I said.

"Maybe," said Robeson dubiously. He made adjustments on the suit controls in his belt, activating the gravitic bonding regulator that we usually used out in space when we had to make inspections or repairs outside our ship; it would provide a paragravity bond between Robeson's suit and anything he touched.

"I'm going up there," he said.

Immediately he went to the base of the strange alien building and began to climb its looming wall. The surface was so rough and irregular that he could almost have climbed it unaided, finding foot- and handholds as he went, but with the paragravity device he went up it like a fly.

Stoddard and I watched silently, hearing his breathing become more labored as he climbed. Bits of sandstone crumbled and fell at our feet, broken loose by his ascent, and we stepped back a bit. When Robeson reached the shadowed niche he stopped, and put a hand into the shadow, and cursed.

"What is it?" I asked.

"Wait a minute." He continued to reach into the opening, feeling about in the darkness. Then he said, "It's another dead end."

"Nothing at all?" I said.

"It's not an opening. It's just a depression, a dent like the spots on dice. It goes in two feet and stops."

He kept probing with his hand for a while, then abruptly he started back down the wall, saying nothing. Stoddard and I looked at each other; Stoddard shrugged.

Robeson alighted from the wall and stood for a few seconds getting his breath; even in the slight gravity of this planet, it wasn't easy climbing up and down a vertical wall two hundred feet high.

Finally he said, "I don't get it. They built something bigger than Notre Dame, but there's no way to get into it." He scowled up at the giant structure.

Stoddard shook his head, grinning. "Hey, that isn't the important thing," he said. "What's important is that we've actually found the remains of an alien civilization. Whether it was one that could send messages to the stars or just a culture at the Stone-Age level, none of that matters. It isn't up to us to figure out everything about them; that'll be done by the anthropologists who'll come after us. We've *done* our job."

He was gesturing excitedly as he talked, and once again I realized how young he was. A youthful dreamer who'd found on his first star trip what the rest of us had been searching for ever since we'd learned how to star hop. No wonder he was happy.

We should have been happy, too, I thought. But I understood Robeson's frustration.

"What we've found are questions," I told Stoddard.

"Maybe we should have expected it, but when you've spent decades searching one star system after another, you start wanting more than questions; you get impatient. We want to *know* something about these people."

Robeson grunted. "Well, it doesn't look like we're going to get our wish," he said. And he turned and led the way back to our hovercraft.

We rose up from the sandstone waste and Robeson put the hovercraft into a slow circle around the huge building. We looked down in silence at the crudely built structure, the rose-tinted parapets enclosing the sketchy balcony around the top. I looked for an entrance off that balcony, but I was no longer hoping to find one, and indeed there was nothing there.

"If only we could have found a *hint* . . ." Robeson muttered.

Stoddard didn't fall into his mood; his youthful elation was still on him. "It's beautiful," he said. "The light makes it glow like a fairy castle."

It *was* strangely beautiful from above, rose-tinted and mysterious. The enormous building seemed tiny now, and its clumsy construction took on a finished aspect that hadn't been apparent from the ground. I found myself sharing Stoddard's dreamy fancies.

"It looks like a sand castle made by a giant," I said.

Robeson's head jerked around, and he stared down at the alien building.

"I'll be damned," he said.

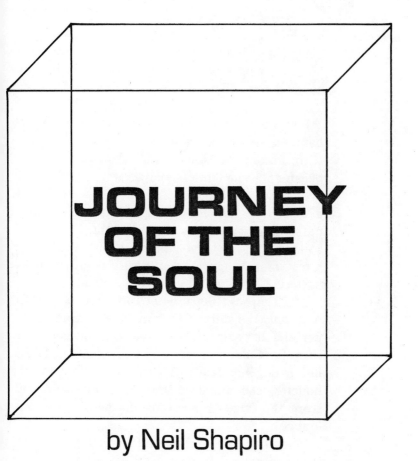

JOURNEY OF THE SOUL

by Neil Shapiro

BETTY GRAY WAS AN EMPRESS and a lady in exile; she had been a tyrant and a despot, although a benevolent and enlightened one. Her crime lay not in having ruled her empire nor even in how she had gone about that task. No, her only crime was the time she picked to live in.

For the chimera of democracy once again haunted otherwise sane men's dreams. Back then, before the first of the Black-Hole Relays began to hasten interstellar traffic, the idea of people somehow governing their own political affairs was not looked upon as ridiculously passé. Democracy was then thought, if you can believe it, to be the coming thing. What empire, what Empress, could survive such mass hysteria?

The Empress Betty Gray rode her exile ship with only the stars of the universe to watch over her and her guards. She rode that starship far from the Golden Throne and knew that she faced not exile, but death. A forlorn shadow in silhouette, she stood in the starlight streaming from the huge viewscreens in the ship's main lounge.

To either side and behind her stood men in colorless uniforms who cradled chromed rifles in their arms. She feared these silent men. Sometimes, in the dark of the ship's night, she would awaken screaming with a dream image of an energy bolt piercing her heart. She did not know her guards. if she had, she would have known there was no reason to fear that kind of death.

The glorious revolution had been one thing to these three men, and to others like them. They had helped to topple the towers of Capital Rorrim and had been in the final siege of Fort Reclaim. Two of the three were well-established heroes in the new pantheon of heroic revolt. Although they abhorred the office she had once held, they couldn't help but respect her. She knew they had a job to do and they knew it had to be done.

The third guard, the youngest, was Provisional Lance Corporal Jorrel. He was a much lesser hero of the revolution and was somewhat in awe of his higher ranking companions.

Betty Gray, as a past Empress, easily recognized the look of duty and devotion to a cause in the hard gazes of the two older men. But there was a softer look, a more confusing one to read, in the eyes of young Jorrel.

"What are your orders?" Betty Gray asked, breaking the silence that had lain between the guards and herself all the first week of the journey.

"To remove you," the first guard answered, "from all possibility of regaining control of a people who are now free and wish to remain so." He was a small and a political man. He lived slogans; he believed them. He had vowed to die for other men's slogans.

"To take you into exile," the second guard said, "by the order of the Provisional High Council." This man followed orders. He was also a man who could give orders. To him orders were a way of delineating reality.

"To guard you," Corporal Jorrel said, "and to see you arrive safely."

"But you won't say where?" She gazed out the viewscreen on a universe she no longer felt entirely able to comprehend.

"My Empress . . ." Jorrel's voice broke off. The other two guards glared, the first guard's knuckles were white where he clenched the silvery sheen of a rifle's stock. Jorrel had suddenly fallen into the old, Royalist, ways of speaking. He was a loyal Provisional, but the habits of a young lifetime can be deeply implanted. He blushed under his companion's glares.

"And just where is my exile to be?" The Empress Gray asked him. "Somehow, in all the confusion, the esteemed judges of the tribunal neglected to mention my final destination."

The first guard, the sloganeer, took Jorrel's arm and whispered into the young man's ear, then marched silently back to his own place of guard.

Jorrel assumed a rigid pose of attention. His eyes seemed to gaze right through Betty Gray.

"So that's the way of it?" she said. "You'll excuse me, gentlemen? I'd like to retire." She wheeled about and looking neither right nor left walked swiftly from the lounge.

Once in her cabin she stretched out on the hard mattress of her cot and stared blankly at the ceiling bulkhead. She tried to tell herself that the rumors could not have been true, but she knew that they were. For the first time, she seriously considered suicide. But the guards had done every part of their job well. There were no knives aboard ship nor anything else with a cutting edge. Her clothing and bedsheets were fashioned of light materials that could not make a noose capable of supporting her weight.

If she had not been an Empress, she might have thought of more original ways to kill herself. But the very idea was so divorced from her upbringing that such originality could hardly be expected of her.

She tried to compose herself for sleep. But whenever she closed her eyes she pictured the fate that she was now certain lay in store for her.

She knew enough of astrogation to tell generally what quadrant of known space they were headed for.

She slept but that was no escape. She dreamed of her coming death, of the black-hole star that fed on space itself and snuffed out light and life.

Charon sat before the banked control boards and sensor readouts, all of which he had designed and built long years ago. Watching them, interpreting them, second-guessing them was by now his second nature. He monitored because he always did so. But it was more than a habit, it was a way of life.

It was the only life he knew and it was just about the only life he could remember except in shadowy recollection. But those shadows were so faded by the intervening years that, for all he could swear to, those memories might never have been realities.

He recalled a tall, hawk-featured man. There was a strength to him and more than a fleeting physical one, there was the powerful aura of a man who had said that he was going to leave everything and go, and who had then actually left.

He had braved death. More than that, he had braved an unknown death. It's quite easy to brave death by fire, or by water, or by anything that experience can name. But to brave a death that cannot be labeled, a death completely unknown, means to die a little just at the thought of it alone.

He rose from the control boards and walked across his throne room to the main computer inputs. Around him the room flickered with lights from instruments which indicated such inconsequentials as oxygen pressure, temperature, food synthesis. Once he had needed machines for such things. He no longer did. But he continued to use them. It was easier. It was another habit.

Charon's kingdom was in Charon's universe. It was his universe by discovery and by right of occupation. It gave him power, complete power, and control. He, in return, supplied it with life—his own life. It was an equitable arrangement and a stable one.

Reaching out his hand, Charon flicked a number of switches on the face of the main computer input. From a small drawer he chose one out of dozens of small, metallic wafers. He inserted the circuit-chip into a small slot on the front of the computer unit.

The air of the room seemed to waver and then it stabilized, now filled with three-dimensional and life-size holographic images.

The images wore early-eighteenth-century costumes. The men were beribboned in powdered white wigs and the images of the women were all well-endowed, with startlingly low-cut cleavages. A strange, old music filled the room and the images began to move mindlessly in an intricate dance and design. Charon joined them.

"Now you," Charon said to one image of a robust eighteenth-century Lady of the Court, "will you minuet with me?" The programmed image danced on by.

Another figure danced its prepatterned way across from him, this one a portly gentleman obviously suffering from the gout.

"Tell me," Charon asked, "to what do you attribute the interconnectivity of the black-hole universe with that of varied and changing points within the more conventional confines of Einsteinian space?" The figure looked at Charon with a blank look of enjoyment and the computer moved it farther along the dance.

A young girl danced holographically before him. He looked in her eyes. She watched a point just beyond his right shoulder. He reached out to her; his hand passed silently through the holographic image that was her only flesh.

Charon cursed and removed the metallic wafer from the computer input. The dance, the music, the dancers faded back into nonreality.

He held the tiny circuit-chip in both hands. For a moment the muscles along his arm tensed as if he would snap the metal wafer in half. Then he angrily replaced the device in the drawer, which he closed with a loud, vicious slam.

"I can't believe," he mumbled under his breath, "that I ever could have cared for the minuet." He strode to the corner of the room, diagonally opposite the control banks. A valved doorway, with the word "airlock" stenciled on it, was before him.

He entered the airlock and closed the inner door behind him. It was a small room, with rows of spacesuits hanging along three of the squared-off walls. He looked neither right nor left at the colorful fabrics, but went directly across to the outer door, which was painted bright red.

He opened it.

He walked into his kingdom, into the universe which was his alone.

He floated because he willed himself to float. He whirled in effortless cartwheeling designs in an alien ether of colored fogs. Light of all colors that came from everywhere and from nowhere in particular coruscated about him. He was in his own element now, he was supreme.

Long ago he had assumed the role of being that universe's Creator, for Charon's universe would align itself to any set system of ordering, of thought. But that game had swiftly passed. He could not create life, though all other powers were his. But the complex and ever-changing patterns of a life-force forever escaped him, and a dead world can arouse no true Creator's pride.

Below him, beneath the mists, was the City. It was the only city in that universe. It was beautiful, in its own way. For Charon had once had a very orderly mind and architecture had appealed to him. Below him, the city was a many-faceted star, its streets and avenues radiated outward from a central point which was the small shuttlecraft that had once brought him out of Einsteinian space.

In its way, it was lovely. Charon kept it as a reminder that he was not a creator but was, at most, an engineer. For the city was dead.

Still, he knew that he wanted it no other way. He was a self-professed hermit. A long time ago he had chosen the prospects of unknown death on the grounds that such might lead him to a perfect hermitage. He had won.

The Empress Betty Gray admitted Corporal Jorrel to her chambers.

"What can I do for you?" she asked him. "Isn't it a bit late for a social call?"

Jorrel looked reluctant to meet her eyes. His head was slightly bowed and he stared at the deck under his feet.

"Sit down, then," she said, motioning him to one of the suspensor chairs that hung in the outer foyer of her cabin. Gratefully, the young soldier accepted.

He looked up at her. Betty Gray imagined that she could see emotions chasing themselves across the boy's features.

There was fear; that she knew. There was uncertainty; there was no mistaking that. But there was yet another emotion, one she could not identify.

"It's tomorrow," the young man told her in low tones, "twelve ship-hours from now."

"Tomorrow," she asked, "I seem to have lost track of the schedule. What is tomorrow?" She deliberately made her voice biting and sarcastic. Jorrel reacted to that even more than she expected. She was surprised at the way he squirmed in his chair, at the flush that spread across his face.

"Tomorrow," the boy explained, "we carry out the terms of your . . . exile."

"Exile?" she asked.

Corporal Jorrel stood up. With a visible effort he forced his eyes to meet her gaze.

"Not exile," he said, "but death. They will call it exile, but it won't be. My Empress, they mean to kill you."

"My Empress?" Betty Gray repeated.

"Just listen," he said hurriedly. "As soon as the ship's Cherenkov Drive is halted we will be within shuttlecraft range of the black-hole star in Lyrae. They plan to place you in a preprogrammed shuttle with all manual controls locked out. The shuttle will take you within the gravitational pull of the black-hole star."

"Well," she said, "that would certainly result in my death. But why like that? I suspected an execution, but why such a dramatic one?"

"Many of your people," Jorrel said, "might be disturbed at news of your execution. But all, or nearly all, of them would accept your exile. When we return to Capital Rorrim we will be placed under truth drugs and will appear on planetwide holovision. We will be asked whether you were exiled or not."

"And so the truth drugs," Betty Gray said, "will insure

the people learning of my death." She hesitated, "And of your crime."

"No," Jorrel said and reseated himself, "not that way at all. You see, not only is the gravitational pull of a black-hole star so strong that not even light can escape from it, but it has another property as well. It is believed that these gravitational forces are so immense that Einsteinian space itself cannot contain them. Cosmologists are now certain that a black-hole star rips open a gateway to another, unknown, universe, outside of our own."

"And I'm expected to live through that dimensional transition?"

"No, you're not expected to live. However, the questions asked us under truth drugs will be phrased in a certain manner. Our answers will make it seem that you've been sent somewhere, to a place we can't reveal. In a way, it will be the truth."

Death, the Empress Betty Gray thought. No matter what form it takes, the same finality results. One way, in the end, is much like another. Yet, she could already seem to feel the first, faint, tuggings of the monstrous black-hole star. She felt sweat on the lines of her palms and was inwardly ashamed of her fear. I am an Empress, she told herself, I must be calm. I don't want to die, she thought.

"My responsibility," Jorrel said, "is to lock out the shuttlecraft's manual controls. I will do that but I will also key the onboard computers to accept the sound of a certain keyword which, when spoken by you, will unlock the controls. There will be a few habitable planets within the shuttlecraft's limited range."

"Why, though? Why would you do this for me?"

"I have to relieve the officer on watch," Jorrel said. "They mustn't suspect me." He strode to the doorway, she accompanied him.

He turned to her. Once more she saw that emotion she couldn't put a name to.

"My Empress," he said, and walked down the hallway.

The two senior guards came for her early in the morning and silently led her out of her cabin to the shuttlecraft launchbay.

They entered the launchbay. It was only then, when she saw Corporal Jorrel, that she began to struggle.

"Lance Corporal Jorrel," the tall man said with a certain note of relish, "has disobeyed orders."

The short guard's statement was more direct. "Jorrel is a traitor. Traitors die."

They forced Betty Gray into a chair in front of the viewscreen that showed Jorrel bound and gagged within the small personnel airlock of the shuttlecraft bay. He was bound crudely with ropes. Betty Gray could see him, but Jorrel could not see her.

"What have you done to him?" she asked.

The two guards ignored her questions. The tall guard stepped before a panel and threw a switch. A low, humming noise was carried through the bulkheads. A green light flickered out and was replaced by a bright red one.

Betty Gray watched the viewscreen. Jorrel was huddled over. For a moment he looked up, directly into the camera and blinked fearful eyes.

"Get it over with," the second guard said.

Another switch was thrown. The outer airlock door swung open onto the glittering stars of deadly space.

Corporal Jorrel, traitor to the Provisional High Council of Capital Rorrim, was whisked out of the airlock and out of life.

The Empress Betty Gray screamed. She put her face into her hands and cried. She hardly felt herself being lifted bodily and carried into a different mode of death, a programmed shuttlecraft. Nor did her numbed mind register the jolt as the shuttlecraft left the starship to take her into fatal exile.

All she could see was a face she hadn't known, the features of a boy she had not understood. All she could feel was a blankness where her feelings should have been.

The shuttlecraft sped on, its Cherenkov Drive carrying her swiftly to a meeting with doom. Somewhere ahead was the monstrosity men called the Black Hole, a wild star that held open a doorway into death—and perhaps beyond.

Again?

Charon stared at the indicators on the panel. He didn't need them, not while in his own universe. But consulting them was a reassuring habit. He didn't need the machines to know that there was a ship, a small one, on the verge of breakthrough from the old universe of Einsteinian space. He knew because he was totally in tune with, in *gestalt* with, the universe which was his.

"A suicide?" he mused. "Might be a poet. Perhaps not. Not even all poets are fools."

Green-lit arabic numerals flickered on the control board. "Forty-five minutes to breakthrough," Charon mumbled.

He rose from the control board and stood before the input bank of the main computer. He took a number of thin metallic wafers from out of the wall drawer and fanned them out like playing cards.

He chose one and inserted it into the computer. The air beside him shimmered and then seemed to coalesce into the shape of an old man. Charon regarded the holographic image, its unkempt and long white beard, its walking stick held in a wrinkled hand, its rags masquerading as clothing, and its unshod feet. Charon laughed at the apparition.

"Why do you laugh?" The image's cataracted eyes searched Charon's features.

"Due to the fact," Charon said, "that you, my Old Advisor, are no more real than any of these others." He waved the fan of metallic wafers.

"In a way," the Old Advisor conceded, "that might be true. Still, if you believe that, then why not destroy me? Why consult me at all?"

"Do you think," Charon said angrily, "that someday I won't destroy you? Perhaps today?" He reached for the edge of the circuit-chip which protruded from the input slot. He calmed himself. His hand returned to his side. "Still," he said, "why shouldn't I continue to make use of all my tools? You are nothing other than an extension of the computer's main memory banks. You may occasionally forget that, but I don't. You are a tool."

"Then use me." The old man shrugged his shoulders and spread his hands.

"Certainly." Charon glanced at the control board where the lit figures had already counted backward to thirty-eight. "Compute this, my Old Advisor. Is the power to withhold life synonymous with the power of causing death? Is murder only an active verb or has it a passive mode as well?"

The Old Advisor's features twisted into a look of surprise. "In your case," he said, "even a theologian might say that your concern arrives a bit late. If you have murdered before, you've done so a hundred times. Yet if your continuing refusal to restructure travelers who break through into this dimension is not murder then why now," he smiled, "should you change your *modus operandi*?"

"Then," Charon shouted, "you tell me that my soul is either completely doomed or completely innocent. You holographic fake. As always, your advice is worse than useless. I say to you that he who does not save a life when the opportunity presents, in fact, kills that life."

"Then," the Old Advisor replied, "you are a mass murderer. Does this knowledge make you feel better or worse?"

Charon again seated himself in front of the control boards. The arabic numerals continued their backward, flickering count. His face was bathed in the subdued green light. Suddenly he cradled his head on his upturned palms. When he spoke, he did so with the voice of a man who has lost himself.

"How do I feel?" Charon said. "I feel lonely. So very lonely."

"So now," the Old Advisor said, "we come to the basic problem of every hermit."

"What should I do?" Though he asked the question of himself, it was the aged Advisor who answered.

"Restructure," was his advice. "Company might be just what you need. Give life while you can. Death can be saved for later."

Charon rose shakily to his feet. Once more he walked to the computer input.

"Perhaps," Charon said, "I will no longer have use for you, if I should now follow your advice."

"Entirely possible," the Old Advisor agreed. "But then again you may never be sure of your own needs, confusing them with your desires."

Charon yanked the metallic wafer from the computer input. The form of the Old Advisor flickered rapidly and faded.

"Your advice," Charon said to the now-empty room, "has been less than excellent, as usual."

For a moment, Charon clenched the wafer tightly in both hands. He flexed his wrists, the wafer seemed to shiver in his grasp. A bit more pressure would crack it. Charon sighed. He replaced the wafer with the others and gently closed the drawer.

He glanced at the control board. The green numerals had already cycled from two-digit numbers to one-digit figures. He hurriedly reseated himself at the controls.

He laughed. It was a strange sound somewhere between a scream and a cry. His shoulders shook and his hands trembled while sweat glistened along his forehead.

His hand settled over the switches that controlled the restructuring devices. The tendons in his hands stood out in tension, making his fingers look like talons. The green numerals changed to red. He moved his hands rapidly across the complex controls.

Charon laughed and cried.

Death is not always final. It can sometimes be no more than a state of mind. Take a slice out of primal darkness and position it to cut off all vision of the world of colors and movement. Concentrate on that stygian blackness. Smell its lack of odor. Feel its nothingness. Think only of the dark.

Betty Gray had not died but she was dead to herself. Unconscious, only her subconscious knew the truth and it wasn't telling. True, she would be resurrected but she would be the last to know.

Her last memory: the shuttlecraft out of control as the first tenuous threads of the gravitational field of the black-hole star took hold. The knowledge that Death himself might as well be pulling her to an irresistible doom.

Her last sensation: of a terrible field of force, gravity, pulling her and her ship madly through an uncaring universe, of sudden gravitational surges and pulses threatening even then to pull her apart.

Her last action: consciousness dropping away to seek the healing balm of a darkness it can comprehend.

Her shuttlecraft carried her unconscious form closer and closer to the mystery of the black-hole star.

The black-hole star, an anomaly even in a universe composed of exceptions to the rule, floats in space, invisible to any observing eye. It began so long ago as a star no less normal, to all appearances, than any other reddish giant. Finally, its helium core was used up and the star collapsed under its own awesome weight. Like a phoenix, finding life in death, its own collapse generated heat, heat for fusion beyond the paltry heats of helium gas. Now the star fed off its own carbon reserves, forming elements higher in atomic number than oxygen, all the way to sodium.

Its fate was one of continued renewal, like a painfully diseased man who cannot quite die. Again, the star collapsed and each collapse resulted in yet more heat, more density, and less volume.

Finally it produced iron atoms as waste materials which collect like dead things deep in the sick star's core. Iron. The dead end, or very nearly.

Once again the star collapsed under its own weight and this time it could end existence in a burst of glory, or cling to life at any cost. At this stage its brothers would become supernovae, bursting apart and scattering their substance throughout space.

But a black-hole star has an evil heart and it thrives on continued collapse. It does not nova, for it must live, it must live at any price. The price it pays is its beauty, its light, and light is the soul of a star.

But a few tiny miles across now, made supremely dense by the sequence of collapses, the core of the star goes beyond the iron fusion and begins to use any and all nuclear reactions.

Suddenly, in a part of a second, the price is paid. The

star winks out. It is now so dense that even the photons of light cannot escape from its surface. It wanted life, it receives a cosmological, living death.

It has become a black-hole star.

Irresistibly, its gravitational field pulls even at the very fabric of Einsteinian space, until our own universe cries out against that terrible pull and the black star becomes a deadly gateway to a second universe that has no name.

Betty Gray is caught in that nearly mythical grip as her shuttlecraft tears madly along, diving down the deepest of gravity wells.

She feels herself being pulled to the forward bulkhead and slammed against it, ignominiously spread-eagled. She screams but the black-hole star does not hear her, she cries to no effect. The pain grows ever more intense and she knows that she is finally helpless.

Once again, unconsciousness overcomes her. As her vision fades, the Empress thanks a god she had never before considered that she will not have to live through the pain of her terrible death, the death of a black-hole star.

Charon sat by the control boards. He moved his hands swiftly along rows of numbered, labeled and complex controls. He mumbled to himself and the formulas sounded akin to incantations.

Slightly behind Charon stood the image called the Old Advisor, whose personality was formed by the computer banks and whose body was projected by holography. Charon felt easier—less lonely—in the image's presence.

"Automatic programming is available for this particular sequence." The Old Advisor said.

Charon did not glance up from the board, "No," he said in lowered tones, "not this. This I do myself." For just a second he permitted himself the luxury of a smile. "I can accept giving death via a programmed card," he said, "but the gift of life should have a more personal touch."

"Have you identified a key cell?" The Advisor asked.

"Of course," Charon replied, attentive to the readouts on the board.

"Then restructure begins?"

"In a few seconds," Charon said. "Unless, of course, you distract me once too often."

"Are you then the Resurrection," the Advisor asked, "and the Light as well?"

"I'll do," Charon answered, "until something better comes along."

The image of the old man laughed.

The minutes quickly passed. To Charon there seemed hardly enough time to do all of the dozens of necessary operations.

He had never planned on becoming a murderer; he had never enjoyed being one. But he had found out that earlier decisions control later ones. All that he had ever asked of the universe—our Einsteinian one—was to be left alone.

Suddenly, Charon pushed himself away from the banked rows of control devices. He regarded the now silent array of lights, meters, and dials.

"Shall I ready the shuttlecraft?" The Old Advisor asked.

"Why?" Charon asked, surprised. "It's not needed. I doubt that it even still functions properly."

"She will be confused," the old man said, "and upset. She will need to be acclimated to her new environment. At first, present her with things she can understand, things that will help her to feel safe and at ease. In a way, she has died once."

Charon looked on the image of the old man. He felt a bitter smile cross his face as he said, "And I am a killer. You remember that."

The Advisor made a mock bow. "Earlier," he said, "I took the liberty of preparing the shuttlecraft."

"There are things," Charon said, "one might say against the concept of self-awareness in computers."

Charon, followed by the Advisor, walked to the shuttle-craft bay. The airlock of the small craft hung open. He could see the flashings of lights from inside the vehicle.

"I assume," Charon said, "this craft will at least appear to be functional?"

"Yes."

"Still," Charon added, "I ought not to let my mind wander?"

"It was more conservative of our resources to have it appear functional than it would have been to actually re-store and repair it."

"You did everything properly," Charon said, "and have anticipated my orders exactly." He climbed the short ladder to the airlock and paused in the hatchway. "There will be two for dinner," he said.

"Ah." The Old Advisor smiled.

Charon began to close the shuttlecraft airlock. "I had better," he said, "get into the habit of doing the expected things—like closing airlocks."

"Exactly." The Old Advisor smiled. "Don't keep the lady waiting," he said. Any reply of Charon's was cut off by the thud of the airlock closing.

The shuttlecraft moved on its launch rollers down the gangway and out into space, though not a normal space.

Charon gently placed the Empress Betty Gray on the couch in the shuttlecraft's small cabin. Then he hurried to open a corroded lock on the small medical cabinet. Finally he was able to remove a preloaded syringe.

He knelt beside Betty Gray's unconscious form and in-jected a few cubic centimeters of the drug directly into a small blue vein on one of her delicately formed wrists. Her breathing became more regular.

"Sorry," Charon said softly, "but it wouldn't have done for you to have been awake before now."

Betty Gray's eyelids fluttered, then opened. Her eyes were gray with points of gold in them.

"Don't worry," Charon told her, "now you're safe."

She tried to rise but fell back onto the couch. Her voice was a bit hoarse at first but gradually softened to normal tones.

"Are you a Royalist?" she asked. "The Provisionals have been put down?"

Charon laughed his denial. For a second, Betty Gray again closed her eyes.

"Are you all right?" Charon asked. He was surprised at his feelings, having forgotten what it felt like to feel solicitous of another's welfare.

"Yes," Betty Gray answered, opening her eyes, "sorry. A headache. I feel very weak."

"It will pass." He turned from her and seated himself at the small and utilitarian controls of the shuttlecraft. Though nearly all of them were inoperative he made quite a show out of working them all in proper sequence.

Betty Gray studied the man at the controls and she wasn't sure that she liked what she saw. She couldn't decide any number of important things. His age, for instance. He looked to be more than thirty in one way, but in other ways he seemed quite younger.

"What is your name?" she asked.

"Charon," he said curtly. He found himself reluctant to turn around and look again into those golden-gray eyes.

"Charon," Betty Gray recited, "was the ferryman whose passengers were the dead." Suddenly she began to tremble and covered her face with her hands. "The black hole," Charon heard her murmur, "so dark."

He went to her side and allowed the nonfuctional controls to fend for themselves. He gently took one of her hands in his own. Ghostly emotions woke echoes of long-dead thoughts within him.

Soon her trembling stopped.

"But I can't be dead," she said, "can I? I think, therefore I am." She laughed. "A young Empress can still quote from her classical education."

"You're safe," Charon told her, "and alive."

"Where are we?" she asked. "This isn't the shuttlecraft that I left in. It's older. It looks like a museum exhibit."

Her voice grew cold. She slipped her hand from Charon's; her bearing was once more royal and distant.

"I demand," she said, "to be told where we are and what your plans are to return me to Capital Rorrim."

Charon, rebuffed, seated himself back at the controls. A new emotion threatened to overcome him.

"Where are we?" the Empress demanded again.

"You're in the Land of Oz," he said angrily. "You've gone Through the Looking Glass. You're about to ride on Ezekiel's Wheel of Fire. You're in a dozen of your old classics all at once. You were dead. Now you're alive and I am beginning to regret *that* decision."

He stood and punched savagely down at one of the few switches that worked on the board. That switch controlled a recent modification to the bulkheads that formed the shuttlecraft's prow. They began to slide slowly open.

Betty Gray screamed. Charon laughed. Betty Gray covered her eyes and huddled on the couch, quaking in fear.

The bulkheads continued to slide apart, opening the interior of the craft to whatever environment was beyond its hull.

"What's wrong?" Charon asked, enjoying her fear.

"You'll kill us," Betty Gray whimpered, "you'll kill us both."

Charon suddenly walked over to her and forced her hands from her eyes so that she would have to look at what the now fully opened bulkheads revealed.

She expected to see the black of space and the silver diamonds of the stars. She expected to feel the horror of explosive decompression. She expected to die.

Instead she saw the realm of one particular ferryman.

It had originally been his plan to ease her into things gradually, to take time out to explain and reassure. But she had angered him.

A strange universe was spread out before her gaze. There were colors that whirled in gay insanity. It was not the blackness of Einsteinian space, it was fog and mist, cloud and light. It was a sight so arresting to the eye that she could do nothing at first but stare. For the colored fogs seemed amorphous in places, solid in others. Shapes and forms were unrecognizable, yet some sort of order seemed to hover just beyond the reach of her mind. It was very beautiful and very frightening.

"Where?" she asked. Her voice was far from being the calm tones of a proper Empress. It seemed to her that her words were a thin stream that flowed past the bulkheads to mingle in that strange colored mist.

Charon took her hand. Once more he was a gentleman. His anger had dissipated as quickly as it had formed. Do you feel any stronger yet?" he asked.

Betty Gray nodded. It was true. She did feel stronger. She felt vital and alive—and curious. She noticed then that the shuttlecraft's controls were no longer illuminated; the cabin light no longer came from the now-dead energy globes and seemed to have no discrete source. She wondered why she wasn't more afraid.

Charon helped her to her feet. She needed his support the first few steps. All at once she realized Charon meant to lead her through the open bulkheads and into that universe of incomprehensible designs. In spite of her curiosity, she pulled back.

"Trust me," Charon said. "It will be easier for you the sooner you get accustomed to things as they are here."

Once more he led her forward and this time she did not resist his lead. They stepped out of the ship and into chaos. Betty Gray felt a sharp, tingling sensation; it was as if all of her senses had been heightened at once.

"In a while," Charon said, "you'll be able to get around on your own."

Betty Gray felt surrounded by colors she could feel. She tasted a million different sounds and she felt the beginnings of a curious power.

The colored mists flew past them both in ever-changing streaks of light. Betty Gray held tight to Charon's hand. She felt herself traveling swiftly with no visible means of doing so. Or it could be, she mused, that it was that universe moving by *them*, that *they* were standing still.

"We're nearly there." Charon said to her over the whistling of winds that were not winds, "Don't be upset at what you see. Very little of it is real. Most of it is but symbological representations of inputs human senses were not made to receive."

Confused, but exhilarated, Betty Gray gave herself over completely to the feeling of flying. They moved like birds in the air and the air was colored fogs.

The mists suddenly parted and revealed the City of Mind. The buildings were of a thousand hues and colors covered over with facades and strung with balustrades of veined marbles. The twisting streets wound their way between towering buildings and they seemed to sparkle as if paved with gems. Bridges of silver threads and golden plankings connected and interconnected the top levels of the shining buildings. The entire city was built on a base of purest pearl-colored mist, like a gigantic cloud.

"This city," Charon told her, "was the first thing I created here. I built it during one of my artistic moods. I've outgrown it since then, but I can't bring myself to destroy it. If I did, I might miss it someday and I could probably never create it again. Still, it is good to keep a reminder of my youth about."

"I think it's lovely," Betty Gray said. "It's the loveliest city I've ever seen."

They drew directly above the center of the city, and Betty Gray saw that it was shaped like a many-pointed star. In the center, where met the jeweled avenues and streets, was a small starship. It was an old ship; its hull was breached in dozens of places and it listed a bit to one side.

"Home," Charon said. He smiled.

Still holding her hand, Charon lowered them both slowly towards the open hatchway of the ancient starship.

"He can't create life, you know. He tried, but he couldn't do it. His mind can't picture the complex infrastructures completely enough."

Betty Gray uncertainly regarded the old man in the small cabin Charon had set aside for her personal use.

"What's going to happen to me?" she asked.

The old man ignored the question and continued, "Charon remains in this small ship, rather than living in the city he created. For in the entire city, until you arrived, he was the only bit of life." The Old Advisor laughed as if at a private joke. "Even the name he picked for himself is a clue to the man. Charon who guards the entrance to the realm of the dead by controlling the only access. For this city is quite dead, as are all of his creations."

The Advisor made to continue his lecture but was interrupted by the opening of the cabin door.

"Charon," the old man said pleasantly, "it is long past etiquette for your first visit."

Charon ignored him and spoke directly to the girl.

"I saved your life," he said to her, "are you aware of that?"

"I am properly grateful." Betty Gray answered.

Charon frightened her; he seemed hawklike, almost predatory.

"My man," Charon pointed to the Old Advisor and couldn't help smiling at his own choice of words, "tells me that you are proud. It appears that you expect me to help you further; to do your bidding, one might nearly say."

Betty Gray stood up. She was a tall, young woman and she drew herself to her full height in what she hoped was a royal bearing. "I am an Empress," she said, "and am hereditary ruler of fifteen populated worlds and five planetary bases."

Charon laughed, harshly and with sarcasm.

"I resurrected you," Charon said, "I rebuilt you from subatomic destruction. I put you back together. I renewed you, I gave you life. And," he continued, "when I gave this second birthing to you I didn't include any hereditary titles for you to wear." Again he laughed and Betty Gray shuddered involuntarily. The man is mad, she thought. "I brought you," Charon said, "from out of your universe and into mine and you can't live here without me."

"What is the word?" The Old Advisor interrupted, musingly, his voice pitched for Charon's ears. "Ah, yes," he said, "now I have it. From the Delta memory banks, vocabulary section, microchip four-hundred-seventy-four. The word is 'magnanimous.'"

"To you I gave self-awareness," Charon reminded the Advisor, "and before I did so you were less than nothing. You were a computer, a tool, nothing more."

"Yes," the Old Advisor said, "and I'm grateful to you, as I'm sure is the young lady. But you still have your limitations. Even here."

"The machine," Charon said, and the Old Advisor gracefully bowed, "will explain to you how you happen to be here. I will expect you in my cabin later tonight."

He turned and, without further words, left Betty Gray's cabin.

"He is insane, isn't he?" Betty Gray said. She was surprised at her own emotions; she felt fear and anger but pity as well.

"If you would allow me the use of a word from my youth," the Old Advisor said, "it is difficult to compute that term. I suppose he is insane. But he is likely much saner than most men in his position would still be."

"Still?" Betty Gray asked.

"One does not age here," the Advisor said. "Aging seems to be a function of the Einsteinian space-time continuum. Since Charon gave a computer—myself—self-awareness, it has been nearly five of your centuries. He has never told me how long he was here before that."

"And how did he get here?" Betty Gray asked. "For that matter, how did I?"

"It is simple," the Old Advisor said, "you were thrown through a black hole."

"But," Betty Gray said, "that would be death."

"That it would be," the old man agreed, "unless the necessary precautions are first invented and applied. True, passage through the gravity well of a black hole from Einsteinian space to here does sunder the subatomic structure of matter. However, for the tiniest fraction of time a pattern still exists. This energy pattern, superimposed on both universes, might be likened to a fossil imprint, but one which is completely three-dimensional and exact. It shows how the matter was arranged before the passage and the exact positioning of all subatomic parts. Now if the subatomic particles were once more assembled, along the lines of this pattern, then the object which underwent dimensional transfer could be restructured."

The Old Advisor smiled. "If perhaps you started with a pattern left by the dissolution of an Empress, then you arrive at a restructured Empress."

"But that," Betty Gray insisted, "is still impossible. First, one would have to pass this restructuring apparatus through the black-hole star. But the black hole would destroy the machine. The logic is circular, it doesn't work."

"So it would be," the old man said, "if that were all there was to it. But if the original machine had been sealed within an energy shell which could not be destroyed by gravitational forces?"

"If such an energy shell were possible," Betty Gray said, "then why use the restructuring machine at all? Why not use only the shell to protect any voyager?"

"The energy involved," the Advisor said, "is terribly inimical to human life, though it is not so to whatever degree of life a machine may be said to possess."

Betty Gray was silent. But for one thing she would have dismissed as foolishness all this talk of dimensional transiting, restructuring, and energy shields. No matter how hard she tried, she could not forget the trip she herself had taken into the black hole. She knew that she must have died, yet she was alive.

"I think," the Advisor said, "anything further should be left to Charon to tell you. He expects to see you later tonight".

"I do not," the Empress Betty Gray said, "answer any summons to a man's chambers."

"No, I don't imagine that is a habit you are accustomed to. Let me say that he is a man who has saved your life. He needs you; for the longest time this man has been slowly dying. Go to him, but don't go as a fearful supplicant or feeling it to be your duty." He smiled, "You need not even go as a woman. Certainly don't go as an Empress. Go to him as a friend."

Betty Gray seated herself. "Leave me alone," she said. "I must have time to decide. Your advice may be proper, yet I have to remember that you are his advisor and not, necessarily, mine."

"Very well." The Old Advisor shrugged his bone-thin shoulders. "But I do believe that by advising you as best I can then I serve him as well." The Advisor paused. "He is lonely, you know."

"Lonely?" Betty Gray asked.

"Yes," the Advisor replied, "it is not a sickness from which only royalty may suffer. He has his amusements, hollow ones. He dances with the holograms and he has sung strange songs to the strains of computed music. But he is an imperfect hermit. He left the universe of men to seek the rewards of solitude. But one should experience a reward before striving mightily to attain it."

"Charon means a lot to you, doesn't he?" Betty Gray asked.

"After all," the old man replied, "he is my creator. While true life was not his to give, he bestowed on me a reasonable facsimile of it. He is warped by guilt and by regret, and now he is in need of something."

"Guilt?" Betty Gray asked.

"You are not the first that Charon could have saved," the Advisor said. "You are only the first that he did. Hundreds of times, I have seen him sitting at the controls of that impossible machine. But he began as a hermit; it is hard for him to admit that he could have made a bad choice. Other people have gone through the black holes."

"And he didn't," Betty Gray hesitated, "restructure the others? That is murderous."

"You shouldn't accuse him," the Old Advisor said. "He has already accused himself, more times than you might believe. But he came here to be a hermit. What hermit needs a population? Besides, he is nearly a god here, where all of this universe's natural laws would be considered quite unnatural within Einsteinian space. Would you ask a hermit to share his lands and a god to share his power?"

"Yes," Betty Gray said decisively, although she admitted to an unsureness within, "I would expect so."

"Then," the old man said, "you are younger than I thought." Going to the doorway he turned and said, "Go to him. Perhaps Charon can explain."

Betty Gray was alone with her thoughts and confusion, alone in a universe she had not yet begun to comprehend.

She knew she would go to Charon later that evening. She wouldn't go because Charon was powerful, nor because he had saved her life, and not for reason of fearing him. She would go to him because he was lonely and that was a thing which an Empress could understand.

"Come in." Charon's voice emanated from a speaker above his cabin door. The door opened automatically and she entered. She found Charon seated at a desk of gleaming alloy in the geometric center of a sparsely furnished room. She seated herself on a chair before the desk, not waiting on an invitation to do so.

"The Advisor," Charon said, "tells me that you were an Empress?"

"I *am* an Empress," Betty Gray said, "though it is true that I have my Empire to regain."

"There is only room here for one member of royalty," Charon said, "and I rule by right."

Betty Gray rose from the chair and curtseyed low before the desk. "I kneel before my liege lord," she said sarcastically.

"Perhaps," Charon calmly replied, "you mistake power for egotism? Would you, beautiful and deposed Empress, like a tour of my realm?"

His calm words struck a note of fear in her. "Perhaps another time," she said, "the hour is now a bit late."

"Follow me." Charon rose and walked to the cabin door and did not look to see if she followed him.

She swallowed outrage as best she could and walked a few steps behind him. She would use him yet, she thought, for all his pride and arrogance.

The old starship was small, though it was a mazelike passage of hallways and elevators, before they arrived at the inner door of the main airlock. Charon stood to one side and motioned Betty Gray to open the airlock and enter it.

She remembered a different airlock. "After you," she said, "as chivalry must take second place to prerogatives of royalty." She tried hard to make her words sound lofty, but trembling nervousness colored her voice.

"We will enter together," Charon said, taking her hand in his, "as befits two of royal blood." He led her into the airlock. Without bothering to seal the inner door, he opened the outer hatchway. The city was spread out before them. Betty Gray looked long at the towers and bridges, the balustrades, the colorful pastels, the gleaming streets and jeweled walkways.

"If you did create this," she said, "you are truthfully an artist. And yet," she added, "I do not see how one man could accomplish all this."

"Quite possible," Charon said, "in my realm. Here, a man's wish is the attainment of the same. Or," he smiled, "a woman's wish."

Once more he grasped Betty Gray's hand and to her repeated astonishment they again rose swiftly into the air.

"It's simple, really," Charon assured her, as their hair was whipped by the breeze their passage created. "One has only to command. We take advantage of natural forces such as lift and drag, though these forces are not caused by any physical action of our own.

"Then again," he said, laughing harshly, "it's hard to say. I gave up formulating theories over a century ago. I found that such theorizing only raised more questions than I could answer."

"But your city," Betty Gray said, "is beautiful." She looked down at the rayed streets below. "For whatever reason."

"It reminds me of the futility of my existence." Charon said. "The city is empty, dead. It will always be that way."

They crossed an invisible divide and the blue of the sky changed to the swirling colors and mists that had been Betty Gray's first sight of Charon's universe.

"This," Charon said with satisfaction, "is my true kingdom."

"It frightens me." Betty Gray replied. The colored fogs beneath her, above her, and to all sides disoriented her. She felt as if she were falling in a dozen directions at once and she no longer had a firm conception of up and down. But it was different from free-fall in Einsteinian space. In this universe, she realized, those directions never existed naturally as there was nothing for them to be relative to.

"There's nothing to fear," Charon said, "although a bit of awe might be suitable. This"—he motioned about them —"is the primal chaos, matter and energy yet unformed, which is so unordered that it will accept the imposition of any ordering at all. Only here, not in your pale universe, may a man express his vaunted creativity."

"Creativity?" Betty Gray questioned. "I don't see opportunity for that here."

"Then you're blind," Charon said, "or you've less intelligence than I thought. The city, what do you expect the city was formed from?"

She was silent. The colors glanced in coruscating waves from her floating form.

"By imposing his orderings on matter and energy," Charon said, "a man creates. In our own universe, creativity is a difficult process. First, a man is forced to conquer a previously established order before he can impose his own. A sculptor must shape and shatter the crystal structure or rock. He has to destroy a basic ordering to impose an order which he calls beauty. An artist must weave the long molecules of his paints onto the pebbled and disorderly surface of his canvas. All men must overcome the physical state of their art. But here there is no order. To impose order onto this canvas calls for no more than the will to do so."

He motioned and about the two of them, the colors seemed to coalesce. The yellows and pastels subtly strengthened, the ochers and the darker colors dissolved.

Suddenly it appeared to Betty Gray that she and Charon were floating in the middle of a hollow but titanically faceted diamond. They were deep within its crystalline walls.

"Anything," Charon told her, "can be created here just by imposing your own will, your own order, your own thoughts onto the dimensional chaos of this universe. "Also—" the huge diamond disappeared back into the mists—"anything once ordered can be destroyed."

"I think I see," Betty Gray said, "but you surely realize that creativity, like any weapon, is not limited to the use of one man alone?"

She focused her entire force of mind on one ordering. She willed her thoughts to impose her own design.

Charon laughed as the colored mists again swirled and

a small dagger of silver plunged toward his chest at a terrible velocity. He pointed at it, with a casual gesture. The dagger's trenchant tip glowed red, then white. The silver began to melt into droplets that dribbled off and dissolved back into the mists.

"It does seem," Charon said, "that you can adapt to situations."

Betty Gray turned from him, shaking with rage. Her anger was not, she realized, due only to the failure of her attack on Charon, but was mostly directed at the ease with which he had parried it.

"Hold!" Charon shouted. She turned and saw Charon's face was dead white; his hands were clenched and sweat beaded on his forehead.

Abruptly, she felt as if she were being squeezed by a giant hand which was dragging her irresistibly through the mists. Spinning wildly about, at the mercy of whatever force was at work on her, she saw that Charon was keeping pace with her just short of a grasping arm's reach.

"What are you doing?" The physical discomfort became pain as her gyrations increased intensity. "Stop it. I can't bear it!"

Charon didn't answer her. As she twirled head over heels she saw that she was leaving him behind her.

She stifled a shout of pure animal terror as she glimpsed what lay ahead of her. Shining and burning through the mists was a blinding orb that might have been the gateway to a medieval hell. Though it was only the size of a pinpoint, its light seemed to devour itself and the space around it. Irresistibly, it drew her closer.

Another force, an opposing one, began to act on her. For a moment she feared that she would be ripped apart. But the second force equalized evenly against the first. Her velocity slowed, her tumbling was gently halted. Once again she hung motionless in the midst of the chaotic colored mists.

A disheveled Charon arrived at her side. "I can hold us both stationary," he said to her, "but it is beyond my mental powers to move us both from its grasp."

"What is it?" she asked. "It's so bright."

"That," Charon told her, "is a black-hole star, as it appears on this side of the dimensional barrier. There wasn't one near to these coordinates recently but distance has no meaning here. Things shift, move about. We are being drawn into it, back into Einsteinian space; but no one is waiting to restructure us on the other side." Charon once more took her hand in his, holding it tightly and protectively in his own. "There's a chance, a small one. Between the two of us, concentrating together, we might be able to move out of its field." He took her into his arms. He kissed her. She was too shocked and too frightened to resist.

"Close your eyes," he told her, "and picture the city and the ship. Imagine the mists taking us there. Impose your will. Impose your own ordering onto this universe. As far as you're concerned, this universe exists only to transport us."

She felt them both begin to move away from that awesome radiance. It could have been a few seconds or a hundred years. Finally, Charon told her that they had succeeded.

She opened her eyes and saw they were again surrounded by the mists. She looked behind her but could catch no glimpse of that hellishly bright effulgence.

She shivered. Charon held her close to him. "It's all right," he said, laughing with relief. "Even my empire occasionally revolts against me." His voice turned hard and he added, "But I always win."

Again they crossed that invisible divide and the mists became a blue sky. The city and the ancient starship were beneath them. They alighted by the airlock of the ship.

"I think," Charon said, "you were right, after all. Another time might have been more suitable for the tour."

Then once more, and again to her surprise, he kissed her. She did not resist.

"Tomorrow," he told her, "we'll have more time. We've all the time in the universe. This universe, of course." He left her in the cabin adjacent to the airlock.

Confused, Betty Gray walked back to her own quarters; there, she seated herself and began to think. Alone in a universe not her own but a universe she could control she thought of Charon. She remembered his kiss. She could still feel it on her lips. She turned her thoughts to means of escaping.

"Do you believe," Betty Gray asked the Old Advisor, "that one person should have the power to limit the freedom of another individual?"

"Allow me to ask my own question. Do you feel one person may use an individual's own property against him?"

Betty Gray was seated at the main control panel but facing the holographic image of the old man.

"No," she said, "not under ordinary circumstances."

"But extraordinary circumstances call for extraordinary morals? Forgive me, Empress, but if I were human I might be tempted to call you ungrateful."

"Ungrateful?" Betty Gray responded scornfully. "Why should I give gratitude to a man who keeps me captive? A prisoner owes his warden nothing, except to attempt escape."

"A prisoner?" The Advisor's tone was puzzled. "If those are the terms you choose, I could give you my own observations on the matter. I may have changed since Charon gave me a modicum of self-awareness, but I can still be objective."

"Talk all day if you'd like." Betty Gray said. "I imagine a thing like you might find lecturing ennobling."

"You mention prisoners," the old man said, unperturbed, "I have seen Charon become your prisoner these past months. He has explained to you all of the machines and more, he has taught you to use the chaos-particles of this universe as well as himself. He has conveniently forgotten that your first free act was to attempt his murder. He overlooks the fact that you speak to him as an Empress to a recalcitrant and dull-witted subject. He has even blinded himself to the fact that all your interest in him and his work is directed only toward finding a means of escape."

"I do," Betty Gray said, "what I have to. You make it sound as if I first pleaded with Charon to keep me here, and only later changed my mind. If, as you are constantly implying, he cares for me, then he would free me. As he won't, I have to attempt it on my own. It is as simple as that."

"You don't understand the very machines you're trying to use. You don't understand Charon and, most of all, you don't understand yourself."

"I understand more than enough," she replied. "I know that in but a few more days I can be out of here and back where I belong."

"You mean back where men gave their very lives to be rid of you?"

She turned to the control board. Her head fell cradled in her arms and her slim shoulders shook as she attempted to stifle the sound of her angry sobs.

"Betty Gray," the Advisor moved closer behind her, "once I told you about Charon. He is lonely, he needs you."

"I have to get away," the Empress said between her tears, "I have to get out of here."

"Why?" the Advisor asked. "What do you fear?"

"Please," she said, "give me just one more day before you tell Charon my plan."

"You still don't understand. I cannot inform Charon of your plans, as it was Charon who told me of them. He instructed me to interfere only if it appeared you were in danger of jeopardizing your own safety."

"What do you mean?"

"I assume," the Advisor said, "that your plan is to send a restructure-module through one of the black-hole gateways and then to follow it?"

"I suppose," Betty Gray said, "that all this was much more obvious than I imagined."

Just then the door to the control cabin opened and Charon entered the room, adding to the anger and fear inside her.

"Thank you," Charon said to the Advisor. "I've been monitoring the conversation. You did allow yourself to wander from what I asked you to say. You see," Charon spoke now to Betty Gray, "I had hoped that you would voluntarily give up your designs. Perhaps I was too proud not to have asked you directly. But now you have forced the issue. You are very close to dangers that you don't understand."

Betty Gray said, "If I exit back through the gateway, which in our home universe is a black-hole star, then I can return to my starting point in Einsteinian space. From there, in a small shuttle, I should be able to reach at least one of the dozen inhabited worlds in the galactic quadrant. You're trying to frighten me into staying. But it won't work, Charon. I will admit that I'm your captive—but only for now."

"You know," Charon said, "or you should know, that this secondary universe is quite different from the one you call home. Not only can its fields be controlled by any ordered framework, no matter how weakly applied, but even concepts of distance and location have no true meaning."

"I've seen that, certainly," Betty Gray admitted. "But what bearing does that have? The black-hole star, that part of it within this dimension, is well within reach."

Rather than answering directly, Charon walked past her to the main control board. With one wrenching pull he snapped the main power switch off the panel.

"Now," he said, holding the broken switch, "you won't be able to kill yourself quite as readily." Ignoring her questions and accusations, Charon left the room.

Betty Gray looked angrily at the Advisor. "Traitor," she said coldly. "I thought you were helping me and all of the time you were a spy. You *are* a machine, a useless and untrustworthy image made in a mockery of life."

"Perhaps so," the Old Advisor said, "but the fact is, I saved your life."

"How did you come to that conclusion? As far as I can see, you merely reassumed your proper role as deputy warden."

"If I were programmed for anger," the old man said, "I think your words would arouse that emotion. However, I will simply say that there are thousands of black-hole stars within the Einsteinian universe. They are hidden in the hearts of nebulae. They are lost in intergalactic voids. They are without number. Without names. Unknown. But each one opens onto the gateway here. Relative positioning is nearly a constant in Einsteinian space but here position has no meaning. If you cross back through the gateway you cannot be at all certain that you will return to the same black-hole star and area around it that you left from.

"The odds," the Advisor continued, "are greatly against even returning to the Milky Way galaxy, let alone to that fraction of one spiral arm which is inhabited by mankind."

"And Charon?" Betty Gray asked as she suddenly began to understand.

"Charon," the Advisor told her, "is as much a prisoner here as you."

"I see. But why didn't Charon tell me this? Was he amused with my escape efforts? Was he pleased to know all my efforts were doomed at inception?"

"You are still an Empress," the Old Advisor said, "and you may remain so for as long as you live; I doubt that you will ever change. I did ask Charon to speak with you, but he said it was his hope you wouldn't try to escape."

"Wouldn't try?" the idea astounded her. "He didn't think I would try to escape?"

"Though Charon could have saved many people, you are the first he restructured. Throughout his life he has believed in such things as loyalty. It was, as I compute it, likely this which led to his becoming a hermit in the first place. Saving you made him regress a bit. You see, he expected you would want to stay."

"Why would I want to stay?"

The Advisor shrugged. "It has been quite some time since Charon had any companionship."

Betty Gray was silent. The old figure of the Advisor turned and left the room. Alone now, in a universe which was both a child's dream and nightmare come true, Betty Gray wondered at the emotions she was feeling.

She seated herself at the control board that the power switch had been torn from. She cried out and brought her small fist down on the surface of the board. Her cry echoed in the small empty room.

Alone with herself, Betty Gray began to lose the first small part of her omnipresent royalty. She cried. Her tears, she told herself, were for an Empire she could never regain. She was a prisoner who cried in a cell from which there could be no escape.

Charon, surrounded by shadow figures, moved to the rhythms of a dance that most of his contemporaries had never heard of. An ancient dance, the minuet, but one reminiscent of the very movements of the stars on their slow and graceful orbits.

Unnoticed at first, the Empress Betty Gray entered the chamber. She watched as the holographic forms bowed and stepped in lifeless gaiety, in nearly hypnotic patterns moved by complex programming.

Charon's eyes were closed and he looked nearly as lifeless as the rest. As the dance brought him closer, Betty Gray impulsively reached out and took hold of his arm. Charon stopped, opened his eyes. The other dancers moved on to the strains of music playing lightly in the air.

"I didn't know," the Empress Betty Gray said to Charon. "You should have told me."

"You would have thought I was lying," Charon told her. "You would have thought I was only trying to keep you here. There is no way back, but one cannot expect an Empress to accept that without proof."

Charon turned from her and walked through the dancing figures; he took no notice of the dancers, nor of the patterns he interrupted. He treated the figures as the shadows they were. At the main input of the computer banks he pulled a thin metallic wafer from the slot. The music ceased abruptly, the dancers halted and then vanished like lights being switched off.

"This," Charon said, and held the wafer out toward Betty Gray, "has been my life." Then, with a quick tensing of his wrists he snapped the wafer in half. As it broke it made a harsh crackling noise. He dropped the two pieces on the floor and ground the microminiaturized circuitry beneath his heel.

He opened a drawer and took out another dozen or more of the wafers. "This one here," he held it up, " is a rather tasteless adaptation of certain myths written down in an old unexpurgated volume of *The Arabian Nights*." He snapped it in half, and laughed. "One may have his computerized dreams, but it seems the reality of such is far beyond my reach."

Charon dashed the rest of the wafers he held to the floor, where they shattered into splintered shards. He took the last wafer from the drawer. He handled it carefully and placed it into the computer input.

The image of the Old Advisor formed in the middle of the room. The form of the old man looked about itself, at Charon and at Betty Gray and at the ruins of the wafers spread out on the deckplates. A slow smile formed on his wrinkled features.

"I am glad," he said to Charon, "that you have forsaken illusion."

"I must," Charon said. "An illusion may be sustained by one man, but it cannot be shared."

"No," the Old Advisor said, "but remember that even as it takes but one man to find illusion, it takes two people to find what is real."

"You are a good friend," Charon said, "but are you real?"

The old man laughed. It was the laughter of a young man, or even a child, amazed at the world around him.

Charon slid the wafer from the computer. The Old Advisor vanished. Charon gazed at the thin metal he held. Then he tensed his wrists and hands along the sides of the wafer.

"Stop," Betty Gray called out, surprising herself as well as Charon. "You can't destroy everything."

"Why not?" Charon asked. "Whatever I create is mine to do with what I want."

"That one creation," Betty Gray said, "has surpassed you, has surpassed us both. To destroy that one would be the same as murder."

"But haven't you heard?" Charon said. "I'm a murderer a hundred times over. You're not the first I could have saved, others blundered through the gateway. But I preferred to live alone, with my illusions. I had everything I needed. One ages so slowly here that immortality seems more than an empty word. Besides, I lived in a universe that begged me to control it, that could be shaped by a man rather than being a shaper of mankind. I came here to escape humanity. Once here I became more than human but something less than that as well."

"You saved me," Betty Gray said. "I'm just now seeing what that cost you."

She walked to his side. She gently took the control wafer from his hands and placed it carefully within the velvet-lined drawer.

"An illusion," she told him, "should always be destroyed. But a friend should never be put aside."

"New friends," he said, "as well as old."

She felt Charon's arms around her.

She drew back and looked into his eyes. She saw hope and happiness there and a brighter, softer emotion as well.

"We can't," Charon told her, "continue to hide here. In time, things would return to how they were. But there would be two people dancing to music with figures that aren't real. We must leave here as soon as we can."

"I'll be with you," Betty Gray said.

"I will prepare protective spheres and restructuring devices. "The gateway will be open to us."

"But where will it lead us?"

"Does that matter?" Charon asked, and Betty Gray knew

that it no longer did. "There are worlds to explore, new experiences to hold. Our home universe is as large as this one is small. No matter where the gateway opens we will be liable to find something worth the trip, something for us to share."

Charon hurried to the main control console. He read the displays.

"The gateway," he said, "will be open for transfer at . . ."

"Tomorrow," Betty Gray said, laughing. She put her arms around him and pulled him back from the controls. "Even the day after. We have all the time in two universes, we can take some of it for ourselves."

She kissed him. Tomorrow, she thought, and ever after.

Soon she would take the journey she had planned, but it would not be in search of her lost Empire, nor would it be a journey of escape.

For Charon who had found that he was again a part of mankind, and for Betty Gray, it would be a journey of the soul.

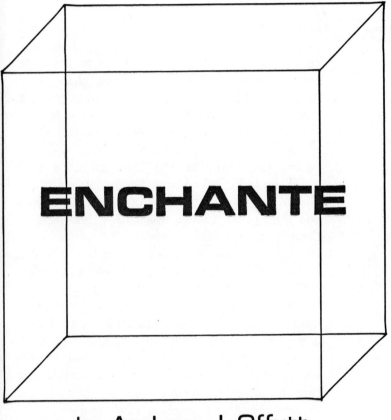

ENCHANTE

by Andrew J. Offutt

WRITHING TENDRILS OF COBWEBS like wraithy fingers seemed to pluck at him in the darkness. The gloom was such that his hand, raised and held before his face, was but a pallid ghost. Fear reached with skeletal fingers sheathed in gray ice.

And then before him stood the sorcerer Bargorjus. His eyes were cinerous holes set in a face old as time: a piece of ancient and yellowed parchment crumpled and then unfolded with wrinkles and cracks intact. From between those deepset ashen eyes his nose fair leaped out, long and thin, to rush down toward his mouth like a thrown spear.

From that lipless gash of a mouth words slid, crackly as the wind-blown dead leaves of autumn.

"You dared what none other has dared," the image said, and a bony finger rose to level at his quaking visitor. "But I promised you one chance, and I keep my word. One chance shall you have, and one only. Henceforth you are a frog, long of leg and hideous of belly and throat, revolting of face. So shall you remain, your kingdom frozen in time, until and unless a fair maid does kiss your repugnant frog's face, in which case you shall return to what you are: a handsome and wealthy prince."

And he laughed, and it was done.

Amid the verdant undergrowth of the Dark Forest dwelt a hideous and popeyed hop toad. He ate, sending forth his tongue to entrap and enfold flies and carry them back to his pendulous frog's belly. Of the fair butterflies, too, he ate, and of the gossamer-winged dragonflies created by the sorcerer that his tormented captive might see beauty, and long for his former life as a man. For now he was but a destroyer of beauty.

He was sad, his man's brain a leaden weight in the loathsome frogform with which he had been cursed.

Too, he was lonely. For there was but one other frog in all the woods, and that a male. They were not friends.

And then on a day like all days, when the insects hummed and the trees rose huge and tall and straight, guardians of the twisted convolvulus of the undergrowth, his life changed once again. Only by chance did he come upon the clearing, and his ugly frog eyes grew even huger, staring.

Fair she was, and lovely, with the shape of a woman and the face of a wise child—and the tip-tilted ears and almond-shaped eyes of a child of the wood. For so she must be: some faerie maid come here in beauty, perhaps the daughter of the King of all Fairies himself.

Long and fine and golden was her hair, a sunny cascade down her back and over her shoulders. Her arms and hands and ears, even her delicate slippers, seemed to drip with blue stones like the dewdrops with which the frog was wont to wash down his insectile breakfast. And her eyes . . . of the same sapphire hue were they, large and lustrous and lovelier than the jewels, for her eyes were not hard, but soft as loving words.

He stared, and he blinked, and tears formed and trickled and rolled from his frog's eyes. She sighed, sitting herself down on the soft earth to gaze straight before her as if mesmerized. Again she sighed, and a dewdrop tear rolled down her cheek from one great wistful eye.

What vast horror had she seen, wondered the frog that was in truth a prince. What sadness could bring such listlessness, such torment to those beautiful eyes, bring such heartrending sighs from that lovely breast?

And he was sad too, sitting quite still to stare at her. He too wept. But no longer was it for his own plight that he shed anguished tears. 'Twas for the sorrow he saw in the eyes of the faerie maiden before him.

At last she rose, and sighed again, and drawing about herself her fringed garb, she went away into the wood. And the frog-prince spent a listless day indeed. Not even the first day of his captivity in this noisome body had been so fraught with misery. He thought only of her perfect beauty. How could such perfection be less than ecstatically happy?

On the morrow he was there at that dewdrop-besprent clearing, and long he waited, and longingly. His joy was ineffable when at last she came, walking with the supple and soft grace of a doe. And it was as it had been on the day previous. She sat, she sighed, she stared at nothing; tears filled her eyes and overflowed to pearl and glisten on her soft cheeks. He gazed at her, but he made neither move nor sound, so that she saw him not. For he had no wish to be seen. He was too hideous. She was too lovely. She was perfection.

For many days was it thus. She, to come and sit and stare at nothing, with sad tears and sadder sighs. And he, to gaze at her in empathy, and sympathy, and love. Aye, love. For within his frog's body there beat the heart of a man, young and handsome, and surely no man could look upon her without love in his heart. It grew, that love, and burgeoned and grew and grew until he was dizzy with its song in his breast.

Many hours of many days passed thus in the clearing in the Dark Forest, with her all unaware of the ugly, yearning eyes turned upon her glowing beauty. Until the day came, and the hour, and then the moment, when she looked up, and he moved not fast enough, and with a little gasp she saw him.

Terrified, he fled, to hide himself for many days, not daring go near the clearing.

But this he could not continue, for there was love and longing in him, and he returned, all silent and small in the darkness beneath the underbrush, and he peered into the clearing—where she sat, as always.

But on this day, she spoke.

"Oh how cruel this enchantment!" she said, in a voice that was all happy birds and silvery streams in the shaded wood and soft womanhood. "How cruel this captivity! And crueler still, to have been given one vision, one hope, and then to have it snatched again from me!" She heaved a great sigh from the high perfection of her maiden's breast.

"O pretty frog that once I saw, where art thou? Am I then to live forever in this place of mocking beauty, and without comfort or companionship?"

The ensorceled one could not believe he heard true. Had she in truth said it? Could it be . . . could it be . . . was she, too, lonely and desirous of company . . . even his company?

. . . until and unless a fair maid does kiss your repugnant frog's face . . .

His heart pounding within him, he crept forth. Without her seeing or hearing he crept from his hiding place, to ease his ungainly body up along a twisted branch that curved nigh to her face. There he perched, to stare at her from a distance of scant inches, and at last it was more than he could bear. He forgot himself, and he opened his mouth to speak to her of his love.

"k'GUNG!"

She turned her head swiftly, hair flying in golden strands like silken threads. Her eyes were wide and round as she gazed upon him, so nearby.

And she smiled.

"Oh," she breathed, her eyes bright, "you handsome creature!"

Then did she sweep his corpulent hideousness up in her hands, and, pressing his coldness against the heat of her bosom, she stroked the crinkly hide of his back. His heart pounded so that he feared it would sunder his chest.

Then she raised him, holding him betwixt her slim hands, and their wide eyes met. What a perfect woman! He stared with mesmerized gaze at her lips, as her hands moved and her lips drew closer, and closer . . .

"What a *perfect* frog," she breathed. And she kissed him.

There was a kaleidoscopic scene-shifting pinwheeling moment of disorientation, and his limbs and skin ached while his brain spun.

And he was a man. The man he had been before, a handsome young prince with lands, and subjects, and wealth, and future. Smiling he turned to his savior, she whom he would make his princess, queen of his heart and his realm.

But she was gone. Weeping he cried out, swinging frantically this way and that in the clearing of ensorcelment. But she was gone. There was only the frog at his feet, a frog smaller than he had been. With great sad eyes it stared in horror at what he had become. He could only stare back, in horror at what she had become. Somewhere, a sorcerer's leaf-crackling voice rose in triumphant and mocking laughter.

For the prince had sought beauty and perfection, and the enchanted lady-frog had sought beauty and perfection, and they had found each other. But beauty is subjective, and true beauty and true perfection are not for men, for they are the work only of Allah, and sorcerers, and artists.

PERI-
HESPERON

by Greg Bear

T WAS THE THREE-HOUR SLEEP PERIOD for the passengers. The corridors were cut by parabolas of light along the walls where the dim lamps glowed orange. The floors were covered with black carpet and reflected no light. The ordinary sounds of shipboard machinery continued. The muted hum of the blowers and the barely audible click-whine of the periodic engine bursts made Karen feel more comfortable, but she was still nervous and a little upset.

Her parents hadn't been in the cabin. She shuffled across the carpet in her blue quilted robe and knitted slippers, her long brown hair quickly combed back behind her ears. As she passed beneath the corridor lights the top of her head glowed in a yellow crescent and her face fell into umber shadow. She reached out to touch the wall for balance, unsteady with the new strength in her step. As planned, the ship's artificial gravity had dropped another quarter since she fell asleep.

Something had scratched the yellow enamel on one wall. She examined the cut for a few seconds, looking at the revealed layers of primer and white undercoating. The plastic bulkhead underneath was gray and the scratch had ripped with the uncertain pressure of whatever had cut it.

"Hello?" she said quietly into an empty cabin.

The door was open and inside the beds were tucked away in the wall. The nets stuck out a little sloppily from their drawer edges and the desk lamp was glowing. She moved on.

The lounge was two decks down. Beneath that was the level reserved for the crew—on this flight three men and two stewardesses. The men were pilots or copilots or whatever they called the people who watched the computerized ship mechanisms, she couldn't recall. The stewardesses were both very young and pretty—Karen had talked to one of them the day before—and maybe they could explain what was going on.

She walked down to the lounge—the central elevator wasn't working—and stood in the doorway with her mouth tight-clenched. Card tables had been drawn out and the theater screen's doors were open. But the chairs were overturned and the cards were scattered as though some wind had blown furiously through the room. A woman's tote bag lay next to a toppled chair, its contents spilled out and something red leaking in a puddle onto the carpet. It was too bright to be blood. She dipped her finger into it and sniffed. Nail polish. Investigating, she found a ruptured aerosol can.

Now she was frightened. With her eyes wide and nostrils flushed with the cold—she was getting sniffles in the chill air—she left the lounge and went into the crew quarters.

"Hello?" she called again. Everybody was gone. The

servoes clicked and whined and a voice spoke from the control room. "Flux rate five thousand hertz, emission velocity point-nine-nine c, time of pulse zero seven-zero-five hours. Request acknowledgement of previous engine analysis."

She stood in the hatchway of the empty control room and listened to the calm chatter of the computer. Beyond the wide transparent panels, stars burned clear and bright. They moved slowly past the window as though the ship were twisting in space. She knew enough about the basic nature of their journey to understand that no such motion was part of the flight plan. The brownish mass of Hesperus moved into view, sparsely striped with ice clouds and gray volcanic smudges. Even from a thousand kilometers the broad crater-scarred roads and cities showed as distinct markings. Her life had vanished with war before man lost his body hair and crossed thumb and little finger.

"Correction rate of thirty-degree axis pitch is one-point-seven kilometers per hour thrust per minute. Correction expected in four minutes seven seconds. Please acknowledge and inform cause of increased pitch. Damage report is incomplete."

The two decks below the crew quarters were for recreation and adjoined a zero-gravity gymnasium. The door to the gymnasium was sealed and the window was fogged with drops of frost. She leaned against the far wall, her lower lip starting to quiver. This is ridiculous, she thought. I'm starting to cry. I will *not* cry. She pushed herself away from the wall and ran around the curving corridor, peering into the automatic galley, empty, and the in-flight storage area. Tears streamed down her cheeks when she completed the inspection and stood again in front of the gymnasium. If they were all inside the closed room, then—

She brightened immediately and pushed the button for the door to open. It stayed shut. The frost on the window slowly cleared and she looked inside. The chamber was a mess. A wide black streak went across the floor and the rubber matting was burned and bubbled. Something was propped against a bulkhead high above the door, a patch of some sort, bulging outward toward the closed-off corridor which ringed the lower level.

"I'll be damned," a low voice said to one side of her. "I thought no one made it." She twisted around to face the man standing a few meters away in the corridor. He wasn't a passenger, she knew immediately, and he wasn't a member of the crew. A stowaway?

"Where is everybody?" she asked, keeping her tone smooth.

"They're gone, honey. Went out like lights a half-hour ago. Were you in your cabin?" She nodded and examined him as though dreaming. He was old and nut-brown. His face was lightly etched with lines and his nose was broad in a way unfamiliar to her. He wore green coveralls and there was an orange lump on his shoulder.

"Where are they?" she asked, not wanting to understand.

"Everybody's dead. I've never seen anything like it. Snuffed out in minutes. Meteoroid took out a man-sized hole in the lower level, and all the doors were jammed open when it plowed through the safety center. She was airless in less than a minute." He pursed his lips and shook his head. "Sorry, honey."

"No," she said, backing away from him. "No!" She ran back along the corridor and up the narrow stairs, hair flying. The man in green stood motionless and looked at where she had stood, his face empty. The lump on his shoulder stirred and extended two horny palps to itch at his ear. "Stop that," he said and the palps withdrew. "We've got more problems than I expected."

When Karen reached her room she looked at the empty nets, still extended, and remembered the card game that had been planned. Her only thought—and part of her coolly considered it ridiculous—was that she was twelve years old and now she was an orphan. What was she going to do?

There was one more body for him to throw out of the ship. Under different circumstances he would have kept the bodies in cold storage, as many as possible, but there was no point in that now. He removed the contorted stewardess's corpse and placed it in the cargo-received lock, closing the inner hatch. He slipped into his spacesuit, adjusted the seals, and opened the three outer hatches. With his hand on the grip-stanchions, he braced himself against the brief flurry of out-rushing air and frozen mist. He kicked the body into space with all his strength and said a brief prayer. Already stiffening from the cold, the body twisted around some mysterious axis and began its slow journey away from the ship.

How was he going to tell the girl what was wrong? He closed the hatch, climbed out of the suit and hung it up neatly in its rack. The orange thing on his shoulder stirred uneasily and he patted it as he restored the elevator to operation, locking off the one ruptured level. He went to find her cabin.

She was sitting on her bed, one hand entwined in the netting, staring at the opposite wall with its screen-picture of terrestrial desert. She turned to look at the old man as he walked into the door frame, then turned back.

"My name's Cammis Alista, Alista my calling name," he said. "What'll I call you?"

She shrugged as if it didn't matter. Then she said, "Karen."

"We've got some trouble, Karen."

"Who are you?" she asked. "I don't remember you on the ship."

"I wasn't," Alista said. "I'm a drifter. Had my own ship,

with Jerk here," pointing at the orange thing, "and saw that your ship was in trouble."

Karen knew enough about interplanetary distances to think that was hardly credible. She shook her head back and forth, trying to show with one part that she was smart enough not to believe him, and with another part that she didn't care.

"I was following your assigned orbit," he said. "Hooked up with your path when you slingshotted around Hesperus to cut travel time to Satiyajit. I was searching for satellites around Hesperus—alien artifacts bring a good price, you know."

She looked at him again, trying to analyze his features, and her eye caught the thing he called Jerk. "Where's your ship?"

"I approached your vessel and didn't keep out of the way of a flux pulse. You were tumbling pretty badly, I thought the computers would have shut down the drive, but you roasted my outer shell like so much cake batter. Got me pretty good, too, with subsidiary scatter." He smiled a weak, meaningless smile at the thought of what that meant.

"I didn't do it," she said.

"I didn't mean you did it, your ship . . ."

"It's not my ship," she said.

"You're right," Alista gave in, shrugging. "It's not really even a ship any more. The safety devices were destroyed and part of the guidance computer. I turned off the engines when I came aboard through the meteor hole. The computer still acts as if the engines were runnning. It clicks its servoes and whistles its little electric songs as though everything were OK. My guess is, about thirty minutes ago we were to start a chain of flux pulses which would establish our path to Satiyajit, but now we're starting to curve back toward Hesperus. The computer put the ship in orbit after the accident, very eccentric, but we'll stay up here all the same." He fell silent and shook his head at his own blabbering. "I'm not insensitive, honey, I know what you're going through . . ." He snapped himself back roughly and ran a hand across his eyes. Drops of water were on the back. Goddamn, he though, I didn't know I was this afraid of dying.

"We're not going to Satiyajit?"

"No chance. Not for a while anyway. They'll be sending ships out soon. They'll be here in a few weeks."

"We'll be alive then?"

He lied. "I don't see why not. Hey, feel like a little food?" She said no and slumped down with her elbows on her knees. She was going to cry now. She knew it with complete certainty and didn't care whether he was there or not. Mother and Father were dead. Why was she alive?

She sobbed once and it shook her softly. The second sob was more violent. Alista couldn't take it. He backed out of the door and said he would fix some food for them. The machines in the automatic galley were in good condition, and he punched up two synthecarn dinners.

Jerk moved restlessly on his shoulder and squeaked its own demands for sustenance. Alista played with the controls of the machines for a moment and came up with a reasonable substitute for a yeast biscuit. He fed this to the animal as he gathered courage to face the girl again.

His lie wouldn't help. Their present orbit would take them right through a belt of Hesperus's moonlets. If they were lucky enough to escape then, in less than a day they'd be running through the belt again. It would be no more than five days before they hit something—probably much sooner. And a rescue ship couldn't approach them for a couple of weeks. He wouldn't live that long anyway. He had no more than three days. Jerk, he thought, could outlast them all by encysting and floating around in the wreckage.

He took the covered trays back to the girl's cabin. Pretending suspicion, she took a morsel from her meal, then ate it slowly, in small bites, while he watched her from the desk chair. Her eyes were puffy. She was very young, he thought. Fourteen, fifteen? Perhaps younger. Girls developed more rapidly in these times. She wasn't what he would call beautiful, but there was a simple regularity about her features which produced a pleasing effect. It was a face which any man could grow to love over the years far more than any rubber-stamp symbol of beauty. "Listen," he said. "You know how to take care of yourself on this thing?"

She nodded as she ate. "Why?"

"I just wanted to know." It wasn't certain that the ship would crack up. "I'm not . . ." But he shook his head and filled his mouth with food. Could he feel the creeping disintegration of his flesh? Would he be hiding himself in a locked sealed cabin the last few hours, so she wouldn't see?

Karen stood up and asked him if he'd picked out a room yet. His look of surprise irritated her. Did he think she was feeling concern? No. She was dead inside. She couldn't be concerned about anything any more.

"Not yet," he said.

"Well, you'd better find one." She wanted to hurt him, tell him—You certainly won't be sleeping *here*—a cruel senseless hurt that would damage her for doing it.

"OK," he said. He took both trays and left, standing in the door frame for a moment, as he had stood before. "You'll be all right, Karen?" His questions were curiously accented in the middle, as though each query were half a statement of fact.

"Yes," she said.

He went to find a cabin and get some sleep.

When he came awake he shut off the inertia field of the net, which had held him in place during the night and kept him warm in the mesh pajamas he'd borrowed. He put everything in its place as though the occupant would be back soon. He had chosen the first officer's cabin, feeling more comfortable in the room of a man who had faced risks as his official duty. If such a man's time came in such a meaningless way, that was his gamble. A passenger's cabin would have made Alista nervous.

He found Karen in the lounge cleaning up the scattered cards and taking out the nail polish with solvent.

"Do you want breakfast?" he asked.

"I've fixed some already," she said.

"I'll get some more myself then."

"Yours is all ready. It's in the warmer."

"Thank you." Looking around the compartment, he commented that it looked better and she shrugged.

"You put them all outside?" she asked.

He nodded.

"Why?"

"Don't ask questions that will hurt you, Karen. I think you understand easily enough."

When he was finished with his food he tapped the orange lump with his finger and it came to life, protruding eyes on stalks and waving palps. "Have you ever seen anything like Jerk before?"

Karen shook her head, no. She didn't want to look at it, or ask any questions, or have it explained to her.

"When I get back from the control room I'll tell you about it. I'm going to shut down the computer and cut the servoes timing the engines. We lose a little battery power each time they go on."

"You stopped the fuel feed?" she asked.

"That I did," Alista said, taking hope from the un-prompted question.

He checked the ship's position by shooting the sun rising over the bloated arc of Hesperus and taking an angle from

Sirius. Comparing his findings with the computer, the machine followed his calculations to three figures. The ship's brains weren't scrambled, then. He threw out his own paper and questioned the guidance systems about their position and orbital velocity. Their speed was increasing and they were approaching Perihesperon. In a few minutes they'd be making their first pass through the lunar belt at—he checked the readout—twenty-two thousand kilometers per hour. At that velocity he had no intention of setting up a dodging pattern on the ship's pitch, yaw, and docking engines.

He didn't feel very old, watching the planets fill the screen. He didn't feel very old at all, but then he couldn't sense the breakdown of his cells either. Flexing his arms, stretching his legs to increase circulation, he felt like a young man, not at all ready to give in.

Something dark blotted out the planet for the blink of an eye. Then a sharply defined scatter of chunks went past. A haze of dust which made the ship tremble and buck. And they were through. First passage.

He returned to the lounge, practicing smiles and wiping them away as they inevitably approached fatuousness.

"Hey!" he said. "I'm going to tell you about Jerk, hmm?"

She nodded, halfway showing interest.

"I picked him up from a dealer on Tau Ceti's Myriadne. He—it—whatever, comes from a place where the air is so bad nothing can breath it, so he breaks down silicates for his oxygen. He eats plants that absorb his own kind when they're dead, and the whole thing . . ." he indicated the ecological pattern with a circling finger, ". . . means that no animal kills another animal to survive. So he's docile and smart . . ." He stopped and didn't feel like saying anything more, but he finished the sentence, "because he absorbs from your own personality, so he's as smart as his owner." Karen was looking at the spot the solvent had made on the carpet. "He, she, it, doesn't matter," Alista said. "Jerk doesn't care."

"Did something happen to you?" she asked. "I mean, when you came near the ship."

Alista felt like a small child who wanted to say something, but couldn't. He was eighty years old and he felt so much like a child that he wanted to find a sympathetic breast and weep. But he was a man long used to death, and finding a frightened weakness in himself made him more reluctant to say or do anything.

"Yes," he said.

"Bad?"

"Yes."

"You're going to die?"

"Yes, dammit! Be quiet. Don't say anything."

And he turned to walk out. A day, two days. That was all.

How long did she have?

The second passage through the belt went smoothly. Alista investigated the emergency buffer shields and used the calculating functions of the computer to see what they could repel. They could handle anything up to nine-tons mass, if they were operating. But they required a safety center to activate them and a guidance system to pinpoint their maximum force on the approaching object. Neither was in good working order. Karen stayed to herself, reading fitfully or trying to sleep, and he stayed in the bridge cabin, idly searching all possible avenues of escape.

If he didn't tell her and she died by surprise, would that be less cruel than telling her? Alista wasn't precisely a religious man, but his Kanaka heritage still impressed him with the idea that dignity and a certain courage in facing one's end led to better relations in the afterlife. Relations to what, he couldn't say—he'd long since stopped thinking about the states or deities beyond death. Death was merely the final solving of mysteries, one way or another.

Karen broke out of her pose of deep self-sorrow when the idea struck her that she wasn't going to survive either. She couldn't shake it because she could visualize nothing beyond the walls of the crippled ship. She went to Alista on the bridge and again the uncomfortable waiting for words began. Alista spoke first, adjusting his seat and manufacturing an excuse to concentrate on the control instruments. "I thought you were asleep."

"Couldn't."

"It'd be good if you could get some rest."

"I've been sleeping for hours," she said. "I've got some more questions."

"Ask them," Alista said.

"What's going to keep the rescue ship from getting here?"

"Nothing."

"Don't lie to me!" she said, indignant. "I'm not a little girl, you know."

"I see," he said. He wanted to ask, And have you had lovers and children, and lost people you loved and understood with the grace of your own years what they had lost by dying?

"It's filthy," she said, "just filthy, not telling me what's going to happen."

"I don't want to make you unhappy."

"I'm not a child," she said softly, evenly.

"You may make it. You'll last longer than I will, anyway. But more than likely the ship will hit a rock in a belt of moonlets and everything will go . . ." with his hands and lips ". . . phht!"

"It will?"

He nodded.

"Goodbye to all, then."

"Hello to what?" he grinned.

"Where are you from?" she asked, And he told her. He talked for a few minutes, telling of old Earth, where she'd never been, of Molokai in a group of islands in a big ocean, of schools and brown children and going away to find the stars were filled with men.

She spoke of her schools on Satiyajit, and the boy friend who was waiting for her, and of her parents. When she could find nothing more to say, she told him how little she had really seen. She was surprised to find she had no more self-pity, only a deep well of honesty which told her all the sad, sad pressure in her gut was something human, of course, but of no use to anybody, least of all her.

They ate dinner together in silence. Alista's face was more relaxed, its lines untensed, and his cheeks less wrinkled. But he was growing paler and weaker. When he was alone in his cabin he vomited up his food and slept fitfully, sweating, on the floor, wrapped in a curtain un-hooked from the lounge wall. He couldn't stand the form-less comfort of the inert bed.

"Let's be a little happy," Karen said when the sleep period was over and she met Alista in the hall around the gymnasium. "Can you make the music operate?" He said he could, but he was too weak to dance. "Then let me dance for you," she said. "You won't mind?"

He could hardly mind. She put on blue tights and tied her long hair beneath her chin, putting a rounded white cap on top of her head. With a clapper in one hand and a bell in the other, she showed him a smooth ballet to or-chestrated concréte sounds. She moved in slow motion in the low gravity, but when she finished her breath came in heavy gasps. Her face, flushed with exertion, showed no awareness of the upcoming third passage.

Alista put himself to bed an hour later and took a small drink of water from a cup brought by Karen. With the weakening of his blood, his face was pale; with the failure of his liver, it was yellowing. He asked her to get him the medicine kit from the medical officer's cabin and she did so. When she came back he saw she'd been crying and he asked her why.

"I can't hold it back," she said. "I just wish I was never born, to have to feel like I do now. It's all so damned useless! I haven't seen or done anything, anything at all!"

"A little while ago you said you weren't a little child. Do you still think that?"

"No," she said. "I feel like I've just been born."

"Would you like to hear a story?" he asked. "Maybe it'll make both of us feel better."

"All right," she said, not sure she wasn't going to be involved in a doddering narrative of old memories.

"I was a gigolo once, a long time ago, and do you know who I was a gigolo to?" Karen shook her head, no. "I was a consort to Baroness Anna Sigrid-Nestor."

"You knew her?" Karen asked, not quite believing. Anna Sigrid-Nestor had been the richest woman in the galaxy, with her control of Dallat Enterprises, the third largest Economische.

"I did. I knew her for three years, the last three years of her life. She was a hundred and fifty years old and she was an abstainer. She didn't use juvenates because—well, I never did find out exactly why she didn't, but even when her doctor told her old age was going to take her out soon, she refused them. She also refused prosthetics and transplants. The last year, I couldn't be her gigolo any more. She finally gave that up." He smiled at the woman's perseverance and Karen managed a grin of half-understanding. "But I stayed on her ship because she liked to talk to me. She had a physician who was too involved with his medical machines to pay her much friendly attention, and everybody else was too scared to come near, so she used

me for that. She kept me on her flagship until she died."
He stopped to regain his breath.

"That damned old woman, do you know what she had
planned for her funeral? She was going to have herself
sealed in a sublight ship when she was dead and shot into
a protostar in the Orion nebula. She thought she could
radiate throughout the galaxy then and be immortal that
way. She contradicted herself by wanting to be immortal
in any way. A few weeks before she died, with the flagship
warping to the nebula, she realized what she was doing
to her beliefs. She wanted to call it off. But she hadn't
been thinking too well, she'd been getting senile—though
I hadn't noticed—and she'd ordered a court-martial of all
the ship's officers if the original mission weren't fulfilled.
Even a personal message in her own voice wouldn't coun-
termand the order, because the flagship had equipment to
create any sort of message a diplomat might need in an
emergency.

"It was insane. She wanted to be buried like everybody
else of her faith, without pretension, and she couldn't.
She told me and I tried to fight the officers, but they
wouldn't budge. They said there was no way out."

"That's horrible," Karen said.

Alista nodded. "We were all waiting for her to die, and
you know what I began to do? Me, tough old Cammis
Alista, I swore I'd never let myself get so involved with
another woman again. You know, she was ugly and
wrinkled and her breasts were dry and flat, but what she'd
been and done; when she was dying, I loved her for those
things. And I wanted to make her live. But there was no
way out." He swallowed. "I talked with her just like you
and I are talking now, and she told me why she had never
wanted to live forever.

" 'Alista,' she said, 'there's something very odd about
living. It's not how long you live, not how long a bird flies,

but how high you reach and what you learn when you get there. Just like a bird that flies as high as it can, and only does it once before going too near the sun. Think of the glory it must feel to go closer than anyone else!' "

He closed his eyes to rest. They were pink with ruptured vessels. "I asked her, 'What if we never get near the sun at all?' And she said that none of us ever do, really, but we have to work to make ourselves think that way. To think that we really do. She said, 'When I last saw the sun, the sun I was born under, it was something I didn't even pay attention to. I didn't care about it. When I last saw the Earth I was rich and young and it didn't matter to me that I might never come back.' The doctor kicked me out of her room, then, no matter what she tried to say to him. But she wrote a note later. When I read it she was dead and they had just shot her off into the protostar cluster."

"What was the note?" Karen asked.

"A poem. I don't know who wrote it, maybe she did. But it said, 'When last I saw my final sun, I was cold and didn't mind the dark. But now, so near, my chill needs your warmth, and I cry for the warmth denied, the dark to come. I want to sing more, say more words, love again.' That was all she wrote."

"Do you know what she meant?"

"No," Alista said. "I still don't. I took juvenates like everybody else. I didn't want to die as she had. When she was gone there was nothing left. A little bit of the dark world came in after her, and she didn't even come to my dreams."

Jerk crawled up from the blankets and squatted on Alista's chest, examining his face carefully with extended eyes.

"I don't want to die either," Karen said. Alista smiled in agreement.

"I'll trade you places, little girl," he said. "I'll take your loneliness for my quick end."

"Maybe I'll be saved," she said. "Maybe we can pass through the ring without hitting anything."

She didn't cry for the old spaceman when he was gone. She walked in a daze to the lounge, taking the limp orange animal with her. She didn't have the strength to write anything down, and it didn't much matter anyway, so she spoke the lines in a soft voice. All the places and things she wanted to see again, and do again, all the people she wanted to meet again.

"There's my parents," she said. Silence. "And Allen. And the school." She tried to understand. "There's the lake at Ankhar, with its snaky blue fish. And my room at . . ."